Gerd Fuchs

THE EMIGRANTS

From Hamburg to the New World

Translated by Heather Hanford

Nobody emigrates without necessity;
Nobody emigrates without hope.
And millions are underway even today.

About this book

Hamburg, 1892. In this year of the cholera epidemic, many people have come together in Hamburg. Whether they know it or not, all of them are on their way to America.

There is the clockmaker Simon Kantor with his wife Ruth and their nine-year-old son Daniel, who escaped a pogrom in the nick of time. They bought their tickets to Hamburg and America from the dazzling (and dubious) character Tatlin, one of HAPAG's emigrant agents. He also procures fake passports and tickets to Hamburg for fugitive Russian army recruits, which is why Prince Rybakov is after him — and why Tatlin himself is fleeing to Hamburg, too. They have to wait at the border station in Eydtkuhnen until Albert Ballin has forced the Hamburg senate to reopen the borders to Russian emigrants.

On the train, they meet Klaus Groth, native of Hamburg and son of a shipyard worker, who is returning to Hamburg following his stint in the army. His mother died of cholera.

The newly licensed physician Albert Werth, scion of an old Sephardic family in Hamburg, lives through the inferno of the cholera epidemic. He turns down an advantageous marriage with the daughter of a Hamburgian banker and decides to serve as a doctor for emigrants instead. This is how he comes to meet the Kantor family, Tatlin, and Groth — as well as Alma Laufer, a nun who has returned to Germany from South-west Africa in order to care for her dying aunt. During her crisis of faith, she falls in love with Werth — and he with her.

About the author

Gerd Fuchs's publications include the novels "Ein Mann fürs Leben", "Stunde Null", "Schinderhannes", "Katharinas Nacht", and "Schußfahrt". He is a member of PEN and lives in Hamburg.

1

It is forbidden to invoke God

Simon Kantor stops the clocks and Igor Tatlin sells him a ticket to paradise. Neighbors.

There are always several who do the hitting. It takes a while until you've beaten someone to death. Until that person is truly dead. And you have to shout while you are dealing the blows. Filthy Jew. Lousy Jew.

He sits amid the ticking of his clocks. He is a clockmaker, and hasn't noticed their ticking anymore for a long time. But not now. Suddenly, he hears it. Rattling, shaking, manifold, yet with machinelike regularity, something is creeping up. Ever closer. Ever louder.

He springs to his feet. This unrelenting rasping fills him with dread. It is midnight. The walls of his workshop are full of clocks. In a moment, they will begin to chime. All of them at once. He stops one pendulum after the other. That's what one does when someone has died. And that is indeed the case. There have been deaths. Seven were beaten to death in the neighboring village yesterday. Old folks and children, too. Once the pogrom spreads to the town, the clockmaker Simon Kantor will be one of the first victims. He has things worth taking.

He brings the last pendulum to a halt as well. Now there is silence. Deep, threatening silence.

He opens the window. The street is still and dark. Glints of chalk-white light in the puddles whenever the clouds part to reveal the moon. He grew up here. Now this town is strange to him. They are permitted to kill him.

The church clock begins to toll. Murderers of our Savior, murderers of children, the priest had preached.

Tatlin works for the Hamburg shipping company HAPAG that has an agency at the border in Eydtkuhnen. HAPAG transports emigrants to America. Tatlin holds speeches about America and the merits of the HAPAG steamships in taverns and inns or just about any place at all. Those who are interested receive forms signed by him that they can present to Mr. Ehrlicher at the agency in Eydtkuhnen. There, they are issued tickets. Tatlin works on a commission basis.

He is large, gaunt. Three sheaths are sewn into the left lining of his frock coat to hold his throwing knives. Sometimes he can be persuaded to throw them at inn doors after anyone who wants to has drawn small circles in chalk on them. And anyone who wants to can tell him how far he has to stand from the door. He always hits his mark. Right on the dot.

Those who emigrate don't do so unless they have to. He only moves on when danger or hunger or despair become too great. So Tatlin has to know where hunger prevails, or danger. Sometimes people call him a vulture. He laughs then, with his blue wolf's eyes in his pockmarked face. He lives in inns and on the road. He has glued a small placard onto his leather shoulder bag. It shows one of the HAPAG steamers with smoke billowing out of its four funnels. Tatlin is in town.

The tolling of the church clock doesn't seem to want to end. Yet after it does, the silence is even deeper, even more threatening. Simon Kantor extinguishes the petroleum lamp and ascends the stairs in the dark. He undresses and slips under the blanket. At once, Ruth is upon him and clings to him. She begins to cry. He holds her close.

Her best friend acted annoyed when she visited her. Claimed she had no time just then. A neighbor called out after her, Jewish slut. Daniel came home from school and said that Natasha, his friend, didn't want to sit next to him anymore. The teacher had laughed and made all the Jewish children sit in the left corner at the back of the classroom.

How are you supposed to explain that to a nine-year-old?

They think they're something special. They're dumb.

But why? We're the ones with the better grades in our report cards.

That's how you know they're dumb.

That isn't a real answer, but Daniel is silent. He knows more than he pretends to know, and he also knows that his father knows more than he lets on. Everyone knows more than they let on.

Weeks ago, Simon Kantor had listened to one of Tatlin's speeches. He had talked about America, land of the free. Wherever Tatlin is present, evil is afoot. Just this morning, he saw him pass by.

Sometimes, when Tatlin talks about America, people ask why he is still here if everything is so wonderful over there. He laughs then and says that he still doesn't have enough money saved for the passage. In fact, he *was* there once before. Yet when he beholds all those hungry, desperate, greedy, trusting faces, he remains silent. It's more lucrative for him that way, too.

He is known for his fearlessness. When asked about that, he laughs and says, I was with the rats. When he was seven, his father shut him down in the cellar for a day on three occasions. After that, he went into the cellar of his own accord. Even at night. His father had trained him to have no fear.

He has a nose for violence. He feels where it is brewing. In the inns and on the street, he hears the words, and in addition and at the same time, hears the tone of voice that accompanies them. He is very successful, because he is always there when it happens. And always beforehand.

He dresses with care. He attaches special importance to his boots. They are custom-made and soft as kid gloves. They make his legs appear even longer than they actually are.

Women throw themselves at him. Above all married ones. But he, too, has a weakness for married women himself. It never ceases to amaze him the risks they are willing to take for the brief time with him on a landing, in a storeroom, in his bed, while the husband, drunk, sleeps next door. Do they do it because they know he will be gone the next day? Because they can dream their dreams through him? It pleases him that he has the power to evoke dreams. But he doesn't know what those dreams are. And they won't tell him. Perhaps because simply uttering it aloud would betray the dream.

He studied for four semesters at the University of Kraków. Mathematics, philosophy, all jumbled together.

In the morning, Simon Kantor goes downstairs to his workshop. There, in the unaccustomed stillness, he suddenly comes to life, remembers what has happened. He immediately starts the pendulums in motion, sets the clocks. Once again, the familiar rasping noise fills the small room. But instead of no longer hearing it after two minutes, he continues to hear it while going about his routine tasks.

He takes up one of the watches in need of repair. After a quarter of an hour, he gives up. He can't concentrate.

Ruth has sent Daniel off to school. Now she sits there and cries.

Those were all neighbors, friends. Have been for generations. Why? Why?

He returns to his workshop. He stares into space. He has got passports, the necessary documents together already. He still hasn't told Ruth about that.

Even by the time Daniel returns home from school, not a single customer has appeared in his workshop. Don't they want their clocks and watches anymore? Or are they going to come and take them for the love of God?

Daniel is upset, but doesn't want to talk. After the midday meal, Simon Kantor goes back to his workshop. He sits there for a while; then he gets up, puts on his coat, and takes his hat from the peg. He opens the door. He is suddenly overcome by fear, a fear of stepping onto the street. He pushes off like a swimmer. He walks with his back straight as a rod. Raises his hat in greeting. Practically nobody greets him in return. They act as if they don't see him. For them, he doesn't even exist anymore.

He goes to Lewinski. He is a baker and lives in one of the side streets. He's looking for a house on the main street.

You made me an offer recently, Kantor says. Are you still interested?

Lewinski looks at him. Flabby jowls; bald head; small, malicious eyes. Lewinski begins to grin and then shakes his head without a word.

It's exactly as if he'd said, I'll get my hands on your house one way or the other, Simon Kantor thinks. He leaves without saying goodbye.

The inn is full. That is very unusual for this time of day. Howling bursts of laughter well up again and again. Kantor has to force himself not to walk faster, or even give in to the urge to run.

He sees Tatlin in front of him. He calls to him. Tatlin comes to a halt.

What does the passage to America cost? Simon Kantor inquires. Two adults, one child. When he hears the price, he says, I'd have to sell my house for that. But nobody wants it anymore.

No problem, Tatlin replies. We have cases like yours all the time. Mr. Ehrlicher, the HAPAG agent, will buy it from you. On the condition that you book the passage. That will then be subtracted from the purchase price.

They enter Simon Kantor's workshop. Tatlin takes forms and brochures out of his shoulder bag.

You need to sign here, and here. Do you know what the Vilna Gaon said?

Simon Kantor looks up.

With the discovery of America, the period of exile is drawing to a close.

Tatlin removes a large, folded paper from his bag and opens it. A steel engraving.

This is an overview of Hamburg. Here are the river Elbe and the ports. There's the city and the lake in the middle of the city, the Alster. The ship departs from this point. Hamburg, that's a little bit of America already, Tatlin says.

Good, says Simon Kantor. I'll think about it.

Daniel is sitting in the kitchen on the bench next to the stove. He stares straight ahead in silence. Now he has the look, too, Simon Kantor thinks. Our look. The look that separates us from the others.

Ruth just cries, unable to think clearly. He will have to make the decision, he alone. He goes into his workshop, spreads out the papers Tatlin left with him on the table, and begins to read. They would have to travel by train to Eydtkuhnen on the Prussian border. In the meantime, Tatlin would have written to this Ehrlicher fellow and informed him about the value of their house. Then the journey would continue by train via Berlin to Hamburg. It is shortly before midnight when Simon Kantor signs the papers.

But that still doesn't mean it's final, he thinks.

Tatlin was twelve when his father gambled away the estate, shot himself, and the new owner had the manor house torn down and a new one built. His mother married her lover, the stationmaster, and Tatlin was sent away to boarding school in Kraków.

Again and again, he would run outside the town to watch them tear down the house. To see how the tiles flew off the roof, and how his hiding places were exposed little by little. How the winding cavities where he had sought refuge and his secret treasure vaults were revealed to the light of day and the fists of the workers. How the big old oak staircase that led upstairs from the vestibule, whose every creaky step he knew by heart, was thrown into the yard and burned. How the pickaxes broke apart the stonework and the rooms stood exposed to the rain. Light-colored spots appeared where pictures once hung. But he didn't see those light-colored spots; he still saw the pictures hanging in their place. And when there was just an empty space left where the house had stood, he noticed that the house had reassembled itself in his head, and that he could wander around it at will like he used to Sundays after the midday meal, when everyone was asleep, with the drawback that he was always twelve years old and alone. Thus he wasn't really without a home. His home was inside him. He carried it around with him.

By dawn, Simon Kantor has made up his mind. He rises and goes downstairs. At his workbench, he writes a letter — to himself. He folds it, puts it in an envelope that he addresses to himself as well, and seals it. Holding an old piece of business correspondence from Germany over the steam of the kettle, he removes the stamp and sticks it onto the envelope. Then he slits open the envelope with his pocketknife. When Ruth comes down with Daniel, he's finished.

Sit down, says Simon Kantor. A letter has arrived.

Daniel's eyes grow larger.

At that age, Simon Kantor thinks, they're still almost like girls.

A letter from Uncle Potjomkin in America. One has to travel by train and then by ship to get there.

Dear Simon, dear Ruth, dear Daniel, Uncle Potjomkin writes, says Simon Kantor. I am ill and in dire need. You must come at once.

Daniel slumps against the back of the chair.

Anyone can say that.

But Daniel. When someone is in need, we must help him. That is our duty as human beings.

And who is helping us? Is that people's duty here, too?

Here, too, Simon Kantor says firmly.

But I don't want to go to America. What kind of difficulty is this Uncle Potjomkin in anyhow?

Simon Kantor had anticipated that appealing to virtue alone would not be enough.

My servants have left me, he continues to read, my race-horses are starving, my automobiles are rusting, and my villa is falling into disrepair.

Daniel has sat up straight again.

You are my only blood relations, and after my death, which surely will not be long in coming, my only heirs. I plan to make Daniel my principal heir, however.

So when do we leave? Daniel says.

13

Tomorrow. And you're not going to school anymore either. You can help Mama with the packing.

The first thing he does is gather up his tools. He had started repairing watches at the young age of fourteen. Some time ago, he had begun with goldsmith's work out of boredom. Naturally, he didn't have any gold or silver to work with, but he did have copper, sheet zinc, iron. He embossed stylized vines and blossoms in sheet copper, complicated ornaments, fruit. The person who adorns himself is a person who values himself, he'd thought. He takes pleasure in himself. He sent for a catalogue from Pforzheim in Germany and ordered a small supply of inexpensive rings, chains, pendants, and earrings that he began to sell in addition to the watches. Whenever the fellows came in with their girlfriends and bought them a ring or a necklace, he always observed the girls, the smile that appeared when they slipped on the ring and looked at their hand. And he saw what took place with their eyes when they tossed back their hair in front of the mirror and tried on an earring. Later on, he became interested in precious stones, jewels, rare gems — mysterious things in which light was transformed into a red or blue or white glow. But he knew that only from his catalogue. He had never seen a real precious stone.

He can still feel the fear, and he realizes that it was always there inside him, rising and falling like old, black groundwater in a cellar. Packing helps relieve the fear. I'm no sheep that allows itself to be slaughtered, he thinks. I'm doing the only thing that's left. But at least I'm doing it. Even though I don't know if what I'm doing is senseless, too.

The newspaper had been fomenting: the Jewish problem, the Jewish peril, the Jewish conspiracy. They commit ritual murders, it claimed, because they need the blood of Christians to make their matzah that they eat during Passover. Supposedly the czar had issued a secret decree that allowed people to treat the Jews however they saw fit. Something new had been added to this fear of the Jews that had spread along with the rumors. Murder was permitted. The police looked on without intervening.

He puts the pocket watches (a few) and the alarm clocks with the tools. He wraps the jewelry in a cloth and puts it with them: cheap rings, a couple of thin silver necklaces, two garnet brooches.

He takes down the wall clocks, unscrews the clockworks, and places them in the suitcase. Then he takes apart the cases and puts these in as well. This is all that he owns, that and the house. The workshop looks as if it has been plundered.

Out on the street, things are restless. There weren't any customers today either. Neither he nor Ruth nor Daniel left the house. From the doorpost, he removes the mezuzah that is attached to the upper third of the frame and tilts toward the room's interior. He takes the parchment scroll inscribed with the words from the fifth book of the Pentateuch (Deuteronomy 6:4–9; 11:13–21) from the small metal case. All that is visible to the observer is the back of the parchment with the word *Shaddai*, Almighty. He smoothes the parchment scroll, folds it, and places it in the suitcase. Now they are ready. Daniel is sleeping in his clothes. Howling and laughter come from the inn. The night lies before them.

It is forbidden to cry.

It is forbidden to look at the clock and to ask questions that begin with Why.

It is one's duty to put on one's good clothes and to polish one's boots and shoes until they gleam as if varnished.

It is forbidden to think about whether they might be spared and if they could perhaps unpack the suitcases.

It is forbidden to invoke God.

It is one's duty to play chess and to want to win.

It is forbidden to look at one another too much, to touch one another, or to kiss one another.

Above all, it is forbidden to look at the clock.

It is one's duty to think about the fact that the laws in America apply to everyone and that they elect their President.

It is one's duty to picture how they will take their picnic basket to one of the many lakes that are in the city of New

York, and how they will spend Sunday afternoon beneath the hanging branches of a willow.

It is especially forbidden to think of siblings, relatives, and friends whom they are leaving behind, and also forbidden to think that one has betrayed them and that one has to feel guilty. Rather, it is one's duty to tell oneself that it would not do anyone any good if they stayed put and were killed along with them, just as it is one's duty to think about the fact that in America, everyone, even the children, wear watches, and that these will need to be repaired.

Laughter and howling still emanate from the inn. They have hidden their baggage on a cart up in the woods behind the house. When they come, Ruth immediately will run out the back door up into the woods. He will follow her with Daniel in his arms. That is what they have agreed upon.

All of a sudden, the howling and laughing die down. It is silent. Usually, when the innkeeper closes for the night, it takes half an hour or so before the last person has said his goodbyes and staggered off. Now, something is different. It is deathly still. In front of the door, a suppressed giggle.

Daniel, says Simon Kantor. Daniel is awake at once. Give me your hand, Daniel, says Simon Kantor. And then they run.

They can hear their front door splinter from the kicks; then they are under cover of darkness and the woods. They stop to listen whether they are being pursued. But they are all busy shouting and laughing and laying waste to the house. Simon and Ruth and Daniel watch them do so from above, from the edge of the forest.

They don't speak; they simply watch. At last, they have ceased their raging and are departing. Simon goes down. No one is there anymore. He fetches Ruth and Daniel. And then they stand there amidst the rubble of their household. It covers the floor ankle-deep.

Young Tatlin had at least had the good fortune that his father was removed before he came home. Yet he still saw the carpet with the brownish red stain. Shortly afterwards, it was taken away and burned and replaced by another one, but for young Tatlin, this brownish red stain soon spread itself out on that one as well, as it did even later in the house in his head, even after he replaced that carpet with a different one. He could exchange as many carpets as he wished — very soon, they all turned brownish red in exactly the same spot.

In the large, rambling house, he and his father generally ran into each other purely by chance. The father, always in a hurry, would wave to him on those occasions. Sometimes he would stop and said, You've grown again. Or: I think one of these days you're going to be quite the handsome fellow. He often bet with him. Want to bet that the lightning will strike the barn over there this time? Should his son lose the bet, which rarely happened, he insisted that he pay up. Betting was serious business for him. And a way of providing his son with an allowance.

Although he seldom saw his father, he didn't have the feeling that he'd forgotten about him. He was convinced that his father thought of him often. Given his haste and the urgency of his business dealings, he was proud that he was able to lend him support by not pestering him with trifling concerns, and that his father was very appreciative of this, so that they were bound to each other like two people who help each other out. Someday, when he was older, his father would bring him along to all these hunting parties, cattle auctions, and dances, of that he was sure.

The occasions when he had shut him in with the rats had nothing to do with his father, but rather with his mother. Supposedly, he had spoken to her in a fresh and disrespectful manner. He'd already forgotten what he was supposed to have said by the time he was pushed down the cellar stairs. His mother was a woman who could, out of the blue, instigate a quarrel that in no time at all had his father arguing dumbfoundedly, and then shouting helplessly. In all likelihood she was just trying to draw attention to herself, since his father paid her as little heed as he did the son, which meant that he only took her accusations seriously because he felt guilty when it came to his wife, whom he of course deceived.

If young Tatlin was convinced that his father hadn't forgotten about him even though he didn't pay him much attention, his mother was quite another story; with her, he got the feeling that for long periods of time, she didn't even know he existed.

One can tell that Tatlin is the son of an estate owner by the way he enters the taproom of a tavern, the way he talks to people: without inhibitions, a little condescendingly, sometimes impatiently, and often somewhat amused. He lives dangerously. The big landowners detest him because he lures cheap workers away from them. And recently he has begun to sell fake passports and ship's passages to Russian deserters. In doing so, he's tangling with the military, or more precisely, with Prince Rybakov, division general. But Tatlin just laughs. Want to bet that the lightning will strike the barn over there this time?

When day breaks, Simon Kantor brings the cart with their baggage down from the woods.

Why? We could have gone to the train station from up there, too, Ruth says.

That's a roundabout route.

But then we have to go through the town.

Then we'll just have to go through the town.

But they won't let us pass. They'll make up for what they didn't get to do last night.

We are going through the town, Simon Kantor shouts. We are going right through the middle of town. That is the first time he has yelled at Ruth.

And thus they set out. Up front, Simon and Daniel were pulling; Ruth pushed from behind. Windows and doors flew open. Children crowded outside. Ruth was glad that she didn't have to walk up front. This way, she was able to lower her head while pushing so she didn't have to see all those faces. Simon and Daniel, however, walked erectly. Head held high and staring straight in front of him, Simon walked along. That is how they departed for town.

18

The children were the first to recover from their surprise. A handful began to follow them, although silent and at a distance that perhaps was so large due to embarrassment. More children joined them, then adolescents, and finally adults. Still they were silent. Simon and Ruth and Daniel could feel this silence; they felt it at their backs.

Don't turn around, said Simon.

They had reached the last of the houses in town. In front of them, they already could see the small wooden building of the train station. A murmuring arose behind them; individual voices called out something; and as the train rounded the hill, they began to shout.

Run, cried Ruth, and pushed with all her might. Simon and Daniel started to run.

They're getting closer, Ruth cried.

The train and the Kantors and their pursuers headed for each other at an acute angle. They would meet at the stationhouse.

Run, cried Ruth.

The Kantors ran; the train chugged closer; it began to brake; and as it came to a halt, they'd reached the platform, although only just ahead of their pursuers. Yet the people on the train must have observed what was going on out there, because the train hadn't even come to a complete standstill before doors were flung open and men jumped down onto the platform. They shoved the three into the compartment, tossed the baggage on afterwards, leapt onto the train themselves, and slammed the doors shut behind them.

The train started off. Cursing and shaking their fists, the mob ran alongside it. Then the platform came to an end; they were left behind; and the faces distorted with rage glided out of view.

Tatlin was eating breakfast at the inn. When he heard voices, he got up and went to the window, and from there he saw the Kantors setting out for town. And he also saw the crowd following them. He returned to the table to continue eating. But he found that he was no longer hungry. He went to the Kantors' house. The splintered door was ajar. It couldn't be closed anymore. He heard voices coming from the kitchen. The baker

Lewinski and his wife were already in the process of determining where to place their furniture.

Do you want to buy this house? Tatlin inquired.

Buy? said Lewinski.

Yes, from the agent Ehrlicher in Eydtkuhnen. He's the one who owns it now.

Lewinski's bald pate began to turn red. He pressed his lips together and was on his way out when Tatlin said, Wait a minute. How very strange, your coat pockets seem to be bulging.

Like a policeman carrying out his familiar routine, he approached him and reached into his pockets.

What have we here? Watches? Pocket watches? Weren't these lying here on the table? Each with a piece of paper noting the names of the owners? Did you want to return them to their owners?

The two left without saying a word.

He sat down at Kantor's workbench; took from his bag paper and indelible pencil; and described for Ehrlicher the house, its location, and its condition; and he also suggested a purchase price. Following that, he went to the mayor, informed him who the new owner was, and deposited the key with him. He also gave him the watches along with the notes indicating the names of their owners.

Finally, he turned his attention to the policeman, the only one in the whole town.

If anything happens to the house, he told him, if for instance it just happens to catch fire, I will hold you personally responsible. This Ehrlicher is not to be trifled with. If I were you, I'd take up my post in front of that house for a couple of hours and inform everyone who the new owner is.

He returned to the inn, paid his bill, and had his horse saddled. At last he could move on. He loves to set out in the morning, when he leaves the houses behind him, then the fields as well; when the uncultivated land commences, brushwood, swamps, forests.

2

Journey of no return, tears of hope

Simon Kantor faints. Good wishes at every station. Poor Doctor Werth.

During the wee hours of August 15, 1892, Dr. Hugo Simon is summoned to a construction worker named Sahling at three a.m., in Prussian-governed Altona near Hamburg. It is Sahling's task to monitor the sewer system's outlet at Klein Grasbrook. As he is returning from work, he is overcome by severe attacks of vomiting and diarrhea. He dies in the early morning hours of August 16. On this day, there were two more cases with the same symptoms. Four occur on August 17, twelve on August 18. By month's end, seven thousand cases have been reported.

On August 29, at six fifteen p.m., Doctor Albert Werth boards the express train to Hamburg in Hanover. After a while, he notices that he is alone in the compartment. He goes into the next one; it is empty as well. He walks through the entire train. He is the only passenger. Apparently, nobody is traveling to Hamburg anymore. The trains that are leaving the city, however, are packed. In the seaside town of Travemünde, well to the north of Hamburg, every single hotel room is booked.

Werth has his license, and three days ago he took his doctor's degree; he is a physician. He is going to Hamburg, his native city, to help fight the epidemic. He has absolutely no experience whatsoever.

It didn't matter how many times he returned to Hamburg — over and over again, he was filled with excitement when the spires of the city appeared and the train crossed the Süderelbe, the southern branch of the river, and then the upper port; when, in the narrower waters of Brooktorhafen, Wandrahmsfleet, and Zollkanal, the ships' superstructures and smokestacks and cranes rose up in front of the Speicherstadt, the warehouse city that seemed to defend the free port of Hamburg like a gigantic fortress wall. St. Nikolai, St. Petri, St. Jacobi, and of course St. Michaelis, or "Michel the Graceful" — it's not as if he actually counted the steeples of these churches, but he made sure of them every time just the same, and they spoke to him. You're home again, they said.

This was important in a city in which there is so much coming and going; a city that opens, down the river Elbe, into the North Sea and out into the Atlantic; a city to which the tide pulses thirty-six miles up the river into the port. A city rich and old, and proud that it never yielded to a sovereign. But now it has covered itself with shame.

The central station stinks. It stinks of Lysol, the agent with which one hopes to disinfect it. Werth takes the streetcar. A woman gets up where the avenue Rothenbaumchaussee begins. With a horrible noise, a stream of liquid feces shoots out from under her skirt. She collapses, vomiting at the same time. A dreadful cloud of stench fills the car. The driver stops with squealing brakes. Together with the conductor, he leaps toward the woman; they pull her from the car, deposit her outside, and jump back on the streetcar. The driver pours water mixed with Lysol from a bucket, which apparently stands at the ready for just such occasions, on the liquid stool, while the conductor pushes it out of the car with a long-handled scrub brush. Both of them are slightly intoxicated. None of the other passengers stirred. Evidently people are used to scenes such as this one.

Werth stands next to the woman who is lying in a heap on the sidewalk. He asks passersby what to do. People tell him he should simply wait until an ambulance comes along. The woman whimpers, vomits. After roughly a quarter of an hour, a coach approaches. Werth jumps into the street and stops it. But it is a hearse. The two drivers are tipsy like the streetcar conductors. (Hard liquor is supposedly a good remedy for cholera, Werth later learns.) Werth gives them five marks to bring the woman to Eppendorf Hospital. They put the woman on top of the two dead bodies, climb up onto the coachbox, and drive off.

Werth walks the rest of the way to Johnsallee. He rings the doorbell of the house where his parents live. The maid ought to come down now and open the door for him. He rings a second, then a third time. He knows his parents are home. The third-story windows are illuminated. When Mrs. Döring, who lives in the apartment above his parents, comes home and unlocks the door, he enters the house with her and ascends the stairs. He rings the bell. Finally, he knocks. After a while he hears footsteps.

There's no one home, Dora calls out from behind the door.

'Tis I, Albert, he says.

The maid opens the door, shrinking away from him at the same time. He walks past her into the parlor. His parents leap to their feet. They want to rush over to him, to hug him as they always do. Yet something holds them back. His mother starts to cry. They stand facing each other. They are helpless.

I haven't touched anything up to now, Werth says.

His father approaches him, wants to embrace him after all. But Albert Werth pulls back.

I don't wish to stay either, he says. I want to go to Eppendorf Hospital. I think they can use me there.

No, his mother cries.

Werth turns around and leaves.

While the hate-filled faces of his pursuers slowly were being left behind and gliding out of view, Simon Kantor fainted. He simply collapsed.

Ruth immediately began to talk wild. They picked him up and placed him on the wooden bench. Ruth wrung her hands over him. A man unbuttoned his vest and the top buttons of his shirt. A woman held her open perfume flacon under his nose. Its contents were such that Simon Kantor opened his eyes at once and sneezed. He sat upright, smiled in embarrassment, and buttoned up his vest and shirt.

I'm better now, he said. And to Ruth: Let me just sit here like this for a while without having to say anything.

He had been a quiet man who would bend over his watches with patience and determination until such point in time when he had found each one's defect. Like a physician during a complicated operation, Ruth thought, and again and again she was impressed by the magnifying glass that he sometimes would wedge in front of his right eye. He was not to be interrupted on any account; he was to be shielded from every disturbance. Above all, he was to be relieved of each and every decision. She practically had him under her thumb.

Now, however, he had yelled at her. For the first time ever. He was filled with a profound sense of shame. But not because of that. He was ashamed that he had run. He was ashamed because of the fear he had felt, because of this cringing fear. And because he had run. In panic and without a shred of dignity.

The shame will stick to him like tar, tenaciously, stubbornly, unable to be removed no matter how hard he tried. He felt soiled.

At the moment, he could only shrug his shoulders about the fear he had experienced when he signed the forms to sell his house; about the fear of embarking on a journey of no return and on a life about which he could neither imagine nor feel anything. He can only hope that this will turn out to be a journey of no return, and as far as this America is concerned: How does it go in that German fairy tale? — We'll find something better than death anywhere.

He puts an arm around Ruth's shoulder, a consoling gesture. But in reality, he would rather receive consolation than give it. She squeezes his hand; she pulls Daniel to her. They always had each other, linked together in shame.

After two nights without sleep, Albert Werth began to reel and sway about. The senior physician sent him to his chamber. He wasn't to show himself again before the following morning.

There are now over a thousand new cases per day. There aren't nearly enough ambulances. Many arrive at the hospital with people who have died along the way. Children are separated from their parents, parents from their children. Many people don't know to which of the two hospitals they have been admitted. There aren't anywhere near enough beds. A field hospital is built; wooden huts are nailed together. The wards hold twice as many patients as they are meant to. The dying, the dead, the screaming, the wheezing, those writhing with cramps lie out in the corridors. Outside the ward, corpses lie in the hallways because nobody comes to pick them up. In the city, planks are used to enclose areas that store the corpses until they can be brought to Ohlsdorf Cemetery, where two hundred and fifty gravediggers are busy digging mass graves in shifts, day and night.

It starts with a vague feeling of indisposition and a slight sensation of numbness. This is followed very soon afterwards by a stage of violent and prolonged attacks of vomiting and diarrhea. The excretions are described as being similar to water in which rice has been boiled. The patient loses up to a quarter of his body fluid; he collapses; his blood thickens; the body can no longer maintain its circulatory functions. The skin becomes bluish and puckered; the eyes recede and look dull; hands and feet become cold as ice. Muscle cramps occur, causing the patient to shudder. Acute dehydration and the loss of vital electrolytes and other dissolved matter lead to heart and kidney failure and, in roughly half of the patients, to death.

All the symptoms can occur within five to twelve hours; usually it takes about three or four days before the final stage is reached.

The terrifying thing about the disease is how suddenly it appears. A man returns home from work to find that his wife and children have been taken to the hospital. A person sits down to dinner, apparently in good health, and never makes it to dessert.

The diarrhea and the vomiting cannot be controlled. They often occur in the presence of other people, an unparalleled humiliation. Finally, the appearance of the dead is simply ghastly. Consumption makes the dying person pale and interesting; a person with typhoid becomes delirious with fever and struggles with death. A person with cholera, though, dies wretchedly in his own excreta, and he can barely be recognized anymore: bluish, contorted, with open, glassy eyes, and open

25

mouth. Just get rid of the thing! Bury it, the sooner the better. There are no touching or heroic tales to be told about this type of death. It has no dignity at all.

Albert Werth calls his parents periodically. No, I'm healthy. No, the disease can only break out if it makes it to the digestive tract, and that can only happen via the mouth. Yes, stomach acid plays a part. In people who are well-nourished, it generally kills the bacillus. This is not the case with those who have an inadequate diet or are undernourished, who have a lower acid content — the poor in other words. No, I'll only be back when it's all over.

At least they dare to speak on the telephone with him. In Magdeburg, someone refused to take a phone call from Hamburg for fear of infection.

He also makes two calls to a young lady who, according to rumor, is his fiancée (who started that anyhow?). He can't talk now, but he'll call her again, he says. He tells her that the second time, too. Then he doesn't call her anymore.

Simon Kantor has a vision. He's in America, has been there for years already, and sees himself as he looks in the mirror. An American is looking at himself. Although there aren't any outward features to mark him as such, Kantor knows at once that the face that peers from the mirror is his all right, but an American one all the same. Experiences that he has yet to go through have left their trace in it, have produced a sort of fine toughness.

He awakens. It's loud in the compartment. The people are excited. In the baggage netting, in the corridors: suitcases, backpacks, bags, baskets. Also violin cases, accordion cases, cases for trumpets, even trombones. Stacks of luggage like during a move.

The train begins to brake. Everyone cranes their neck to get a glimpse of the station sign. Things are getting louder, but outside it's loud as well. A crowd of people is making its way down the hill and toward the train station. At the forefront is a voluminous woman. Evidently she is being brought to the train. Yet it appears that she can barely walk. Two women are supporting her; they guide her, hold her, push her forwards. The woman herself has leaned backwards. With her face turned to the clouds, she emits long, lamenting cries. Three children cling to her skirts. Naturally, they are crying. Those around her answer her wails of lament with their own cries. If the throng of people bringing her to the train accounts for half the village, then the bunch waiting for her at the train must be the other half. Is this a funeral, or is it a triumphal procession?

On the platform, the shouts and cries escalate into an uproar. Take care of yourself, Marja. Write at once, Marja. Don't lose the tickets, Marja. Have a good trip. God will protect you. Farewell. Don't forget us.

The stationmaster blows his whistle like mad. The engineer doesn't have the slightest intention of departing. The door is flung open and Marja is shoved on board together with the baggage and children. People manage to shut the door with effort. At last, the train begins to move.

It's as if Marja is in a frenzy. How am I supposed to find him, she shouts, among all those people in New York? He'll be there to meet the train, they call to her. Take heart, Marja.

And all the policemen, Marja calls out, all the conductors, all the sailors, who is going to protect a poor woman like me with three children? We will, they all shouted together. We'll be with you, Marja.

And the sea? Marja calls out. What about the sea? God will protect us, the compartment replies.

Marja is comforted from all sides. Marja needs consoling; and thus, things quiet down somewhat, but that only makes the sobs of a man, who had been shoved into the compartment with Marja unseen, all the more noticeable.

I have to leave behind everything, he sobs. A wife and five children.

They'll come later, like Marja, they call to him.

My brothers, my sister, my mother, my own flesh and blood — I'm losing everything. They'll all come later, they exclaim.

And how am I supposed to tell anyone what my name is? I can't speak the language. Every American speaks Russian, German, and Yiddish, they exclaim.

The agitation mounts from station to station. A woman with two children hasn't heard from her husband in two years. She's going to New York to look for him. She doesn't have an address. A man wanted to return to collect his wife and children. But she has found someone else. Now he's going back. Entire families have tickets only as far as Eydtkuhnen. These are *Luftmenschen*, people of air; half the compartment consists of people of air. People of air don't have a job. They deal in apparently worthless stuff. People of air live from day to day, from hour to hour even.

And how do you plan to get any farther with no money? God will have mercy on us.

Two young Russian country lads sit silent and stockstill in the midst of this commotion. They don't know that an American farmhand earns four times that of a Russian farm worker. That the wheat yield on a hundred ares is 15 centners in America; 23 in Germany; 38 in Great Britain; 53 in Denmark; but where they're from, only seven and a half centners. All they know is that the estates of the kulaks kept getting bigger and bigger, and that there's less and less land left over for them, while the number of their children and the taxes they owe continue to grow. Most of the Russian small farmers emigrate to Siberia. But they want to go west, to America.

The next station draws closer. Suddenly, they're quiet. They're pricking up their ears because they can hear music, the playing of a brass band, and as the train comes to a halt, another train, coming from the other direction, stops on the opposite track. Here they aren't saying goodbye; here they're welcoming someone. An enormous crowd has gathered. The first-class compartment grinds to a halt directly in front of the brass band. The band stops playing; a girls' choir steps forward. Expectant silence. And then the door to the compartment flies open. In it stands the son who's returned home, the uncle from America.

An immense coat of silver-gray wolf's fur envelopes him. On his head perches a high, white hat with a broad brim. On his feet are pointy boots studded with silver nails. In his left hand he balances a cigar.

The teacher waves his arms; the girls' choir begins its greeting hymn. The photographer ducks under his black cloth, and only after there's been a flash and a tiny puff of smoke rises does the man who's come home descend the stairs. They make room for him in awe as the first thing he does is stride with open, flowing furs toward two wizened little old beings; he embraces and kisses them, they who begot him all those years ago. The girls' choir continues to rejoice. A maid of honor, dressed from head to toe in white, offers him the traditional bread and salt. The mayor tries to begin his speech, but an outcry passes through the crowd.

There, in the door of the first-class compartment, stands a vision. It is dressed in gray, gold-braided livery, yet it is black on its head and hands. A person? Perhaps; at least, the creature laughs like a person, broadly, with a red tongue and flashing white teeth. And it appears to be rational. It adroitly hands the American's baggage from the compartment: suitcases made of the skin of crocodiles, goats, or buffalo, some as big as a cupboard. Boxing gloves; a container type of thing that can be moved about on wheels full of sticks that have a spoonlike attachment on one end; hatboxes. At last, because the train has begun to move, it hops springily onto the platform. The train keeps going, leaving behind one carriage. It has been uncoupled, and on this carriage is something that surpasses everything else they've witnessed thus far.

Upon this carriage, as if upon a throne, triumphs *an automobile*.

Frog-green and polished to a shine, with snow-white tires, flashing chrome spokes, two mighty headlights, and a horn on the side that can be made to squawk via a rubber ball located on its upper end.

A construction that has apparently been prefabricated is hauled up to the carriage, and the ropes that held the frog-green beauty in place during the journey are undone; the black man attaches a handle to the front end, cranks it around with lightning speed two, three times, and then there's a bang. Up front, the automobile begins to vibrate; at the rear end, it emits smoke. The black man sits down behind the wheel, dons his official cap, and the vehicle slowly rolls onto the platform. The baggage is loaded onto it. The two old folks take a seat in front, the American in back, and then, after the photographer lets off another flash, the procession forms. Leading the way is the brass band, which gets to play again after all, then the automobile with the waving American, then the girls' choir, and finally the rest of them waving their hats about enthusiastically.

They had looked on, breathless and silent. They come to life when the train starts up again with a hard jolt. They look at each other. They look at each other in disbelief; they look at each other full of enthusiasm. Yes, that was it indeed. That's how it would be. Each and every one of them would have an automobile. And with that, the compartment starts to sing. Some of them cry, but even through their tears, they sing along; the whole train is singing. They would be saved. They thank the Almighty. A small, rattletrap train that rolls across a wide, treeless plain. But a train that sings.

Many trains have rolled along like that before this one, and many more will follow.

In Eydtkuhnen, Simon Kantor takes Ruth and Daniel to the station restaurant, then he makes his way to the HAPAG agency.

You do know that the border is closed, says Ehrlicher.

Simon Kantor stares at the fat fellow.

Tatlin didn't say a word about that.

Ehrlicher shrugs his shoulders and laughs. They've got cholera in Hamburg.

On August 22, Hamburg senator Hachmann had given orders for all emigrants arriving from Russia to be interned in the huts located at the America quay. On August 24, Robert Koch, the man who discovered the cholera bacillus, inspected the huts and declared that the cause of the epidemic probably was to be found there. On August 29, the Prussian border is closed to Russian emigrants who don't have tickets or who only have tickets for the steerage class. At the beginning of September, HAPAG shuts down the passage to America via steerage entirely. Travelers with tickets for the cabin deck or first class are allowed to cross. Evidently the germ is capable of differentiating according to tickets.

3

Tatlin's secret

He is seduced and he takes part in a battue.
He throws his knives.

That could be them, Tatlin thinks. Two young fellows have entered the taproom. They look around as if they're looking for seats. There are plenty of those, and unoccupied tables as well. Here? says one of them, and points to a free table. But the other one keeps going as if he didn't hear anything. They are coming closer.

That has to be them, Tatlin thinks. They stop at his table. May we take a seat? inquires one of them.

Please do, Tatlin replies. He has to suppress a smile.

Relieved, they sit down. The larger one rubs his hands together as if he needs to warm them. However, the gesture could also signal satisfaction, even anticipation.

Got cold, Tatlin says.

The larger one agrees with him in relief. There's already been frost at night, he assures him. They talk about the weather and wonder if they have a hard winter before them.

How do you recognize an informer? You don't, Tatlin thinks. At least, not right away. He looks at their faces and thinks, They're young, they're the right age. Sons of farmers. Tatlin waits. At long last, the smaller of the two men makes the first move.

He's heard that two of his comrades didn't return from leave. That they've taken off, wanted to go to America. What a couple of dummies. As if that's possible.

Tatlin can't help smiling. He tilts his head.

That would depend. What were their names?

We don't know. But is that even possible, that they could make it? To America?

Well, first of all, they'd need papers. Different ones. New

ones, Tatlin says. Otherwise, they'd get stuck at the border, or at the very latest in Hamburg, when they try to board the ship.

Right about now would be the time for them to mention the name Krishin, Tatlin thinks.

The two look at each other. The larger one finally takes the plunge.

That's what Krishin says, too, he states.

Tatlin is just about to lean back in relaxation when the forester enters the taproom. The forester of the prince, General Rybakov's forester. He heads for Tatlin's table.

How much longer are you on leave?

We have to be on our way at nine, the smaller one replies.

Do you have the money with you? They nod. In a moment, I'm going to say that I'm going to bed. You two remain seated. I'll be back later.

The forester has reached their table. He shakes Tatlin's hand with great heartiness. Three weeks ago, Tatlin cuckolded him. And he knows it. His pleasure at seeing Tatlin again is immense. The great battue that the prince holds every year is upon us, he says.

Suddenly, he turns to the two young men.

Is your company taking part in the hunt?

When does the battue take place? Tatlin asks. He wants to prevent them from answering, but the smaller one already has said yes.

In saying that, he also has said that he is a recruit in Rybakov's regiment.

The forester, for his part, has given Tatlin to understand that he knows the purpose of his meeting with the two men.

The forester, now in an exceptionally good mood, turns to Tatlin again. In one week's time, he says; and all of a sudden, he has an idea.

I could use a reliable man to direct one of the lines of beaters, he says with a smile. Wouldn't you like to take that on?

Actually, it wasn't Tatlin who had made a cuckold of the forester. It was his wife.

And then we're all invited to the big celebration in the evening, the forester says.

During the course of a battue (a type of hunt in which lines of beaters hit the ground and brush to flush game toward waiting standers), there are shots, many shots, and nobody really can tell from whence and whom they originate. And time and again, it so happens that instead of shooting the game, one of the hunters is hit. By accident.

Rybakov's hunting festivities are famous, the forester says. Tatlin looks him in the eye and says, Yes. That could be a great deal of fun.

Excellent, the forester calls out, slapping him on the back. Thursday at three at the prince's hunting lodge it is then. I'm counting on you.

I believe I have to turn in now, Tatlin says, getting up. The forester stands up as well. It's been a long day, I want to go home. They shake hands at the bar near the door.

Tatlin goes up to his room. He lights the petroleum lamp, waits as long as it takes to undress oneself and get into bed, and then extinguishes it. He goes over to the window. He was right. Down below, in the shadows, stands the forester. He is peering into the illuminated taproom where the two recruits are sitting. He's waiting for Tatlin to come down and finish their business that was interrupted. He wants to catch him in the act. Tatlin grins.

It was pouring, back then; it was getting dark; his horse was lame; it had lost its left hind horseshoe; and that's when he turned off the high road and rode to the forester's house. He was given something to eat; after that, they drank together, and then he went up to the partition in which the forester's wife had laid out a straw mattress and blanket for him.

He woke up during the night. Someone was standing in the room. It was pitch dark. It was quiet. But someone was there. He could feel it.

What compels a mother of two — and her period was late yet again — a woman who toils for sixteen hours a day, seven days a week, what compels a woman like that to go to bed with some Johnny-come-lately whom she doesn't know and who will be gone again the following day?

Come here, he said.

34

Afterwards, they lay there in silence, she in his arms, pressed up close to him. All was still. But then, at a distance, a floorboard creaked.

It was never like that before with a man, she said. But was that what mattered to her? Perhaps she could only express what mattered to her like that. But what did matter to her? What did tears mean to her? Ones that flowed so silently.

Her husband was still asleep when he set out. She was in the process of making a fire in the stove when Tatlin came downstairs.

Leave quickly, she said. And make sure that you never run into that man up there again.

For the man now standing down there, this was taking a bit too long. He mounts his horse and rides off. Tatlin waits a little longer, since he could always decide to return, and then he goes downstairs.

These are your new papers, he says. Can you read? Yes, says the smaller one. Here's what you are called now, here is when you were born, here is the name of the village where you come from, says Tatlin. You have to learn that by heart. You musn't ride on the train, and you musn't encounter any policemen. In Eydtkuhnen, take these papers to a Mr. Ehrlicher in the HAPAG agency. There you will be issued tickets.

The smaller man pushes an envelope with the money across the table to him.

They're going to figure out what's happened in an hour. You know what they do with deserters.

Now Tatlin really can go to sleep.

A year and a half ago, he, too, went to America. After one year, he was back. He was supposed to go on ahead. After a period of orientation, he would send her tickets. Until then, they were going to write each other letters sent general delivery. That was how they had planned it. Her letters in reply to his grew less and less frequent. Finally, they stopped coming entirely. That's when he went back.

Tatlin is walking along in the line of beaters. They are slowly making their way through bushes and thinly wooded areas down into the valley, toward the opposite wall of rock. Later on, under Tatlin's direction, part of the line of beaters is supposed to pivot, block off the route leading up and out of the valley, and, together with the other beaters, drive the game down the valley and in front of the rifles of the prince and his guests. Most of the beaters are recruits, but there are also farmers from the surrounding villages present. They are carrying sticks and clubs with which they will beat the bushes and trees to drive the game from cover.

Next to Tatlin is Ivan, an old man who used to work on his father's estate way back when. Tatlin could not prevent him from coming up close to him.

What did you do to the forester to make him hate you so? Ivan asks.

Tatlin laughs. Did he not invite me here? How, then, could he possibly hate me?

I heard him talking about you, Ivan says. I saw his eyes. Soon there will be shots, many shots, and people won't be able to tell who fired what and which rifle let off the one that hits you.

Let's just see what happens, says Tatlin. Maybe he'll shoot, maybe he won't. Maybe he'll hit me, maybe he won't.

Is your life worth so little to you that you play with it like that? Ivan says. That's an even graver sin than if you took it yourself.

Leave me alone, old man, Tatlin says. But he had allowed Ivan to make his way up next to him in the line.

It is a clear, cold late autumn day. A small, glittering sun already hangs low over the western horizon. Following the first frosts of the season, the foliage glows in shades of deep brown and red. Tatlin is in high spirits. He hopes that he still has time for one thought when his body is struck. That he can still think: There you are at last, Master. I've managed to lure you out of your ambush. You who uses the most ridiculous of coincidences as a pretext: a falling stone, the kick of a horse, cholera, the knife of a drunken man.

She was the daughter of a newspaper publisher, and therefore unattainable for one like him. They met in secret, as if in a fever every time. Only in America did he realize that he would never be able to free himself from her. He was cold in her presence, and got colder still the more she got herself worked up over these fantasies about the incredible adventures she would experience with him, fantasies that plainly had their origin in dime novels. She was small, fragile; he felt sorry for her. He found her repulsive, yet he was at her command.

The forester walks the length of the line of beaters. He takes his place next to Tatlin. A beautiful day, he says, and offers Tatlin a sip from his silver flask. Tatlin drinks and hands it back to him with a smile. Rifle slung over his shoulder, the forester continues on his way with a smile of his own.

There you have it, old man, says Tatlin. He's my friend.

Don't act stupider than you are, Ivan says. He has known Tatlin since childhood, ever since Tatlin was six and he had lifted him up onto one of the two nags he used to bring in the hay — a scrawny little boy who hardly ever spoke and who developed a wordless attachment to him. Who brought him half-smoked cigars from his father's ashtray, or bottles of vodka that had already been opened. Who was satisfied just to be in his presence and to watch him.

They keep flushing out more and more game that breaks through the bushes and flees noisily down into the valley. Sin, Tatlin thinks. What is sin? How many pogroms had he witnessed? How many times had he seen the lust to kill germinate beneath the words, until it broke through and flashed from their eyes, until the first fire sparked the roaring frenzy? How long it takes to beat someone to death. It's not that easy, that much he had found out. One always has to come back and kick them some more. He had stood by, hands in his pockets.

The wall of rock that borders the valley glows in the evening sun, a brown- and gold-marbled surface with an uneven texture. Bluish shadows already nest in the crevices. The curved ridge is trimmed with pine trees. They stand out, black and sharp as a silhouette, against the pale blue evening sky.

Why not now? Tatlin thinks. Why wait so long?

You can still turn back, Ivan says. He hears Tatlin burst out laughing, and he knows that words can't reach him anymore. Just like they couldn't reach the skinny, constantly hungry twelve-year-old who restlessly wandered about the yard like he was looking for something that he himself couldn't put his finger on; who didn't listen to anyone anymore; who acted as if people were speaking in a foreign language to him. He eventually taught him how to throw knives.

Tatlin walks along the line of beaters. He initiates the pivot maneuver. The beaters begin to hit the bushes and trees with their clubs. The forester is at Tatlin's back. He thinks Tatlin hasn't seen him.

The lines of beaters almost have reached the valley floor. Soon the first shots will ring out.

The screams that take place when the murdering starts. Why don't they kill in silence? Why do they have to scream at the same time? Are they trying to fill themselves with courage, or are they screaming out of despair over themselves? Blood squirts from nose and mouth and ears. It marks the murderers.

The wall of rock glows. It can't be much longer now — and then the first shot is fired at last. At once volleys erupt along the entire length of the woodside. A bullet flies by Tatlin's head and lodges in a tree trunk. The bark spurts. The beaters begin to yell. The valley floor is teeming with animals. Stags, wild boar, does, hares, and in between: foxes, badgers, bears. The beaters stop behind the standers who are shooting. Only Tatlin's line continues to move down the valley. They're walking out in the open now. A bullet whistles past Tatlin's ear. In all that screaming and cracking of gunfire, nobody knows who's shooting where.

Tatlin is now entirely unprotected. He sings. He emits long, undulating cries. The wall of rock glows in the dying light. The evening star beams coldly above it. Something slaps against his hip. A bullet has lodged in his shoulder bag. Then he is beyond the range of the rifles. Everywhere there are dead, perishing, fleeing animals, some of which are able to break through the line of beaters.

All of a sudden, the forester is there. Tatlin's beaters are to surround a stag, a mighty nine-pronger. They are to drive it toward the princess. They are able to form a circle around the beast. The stag rushes around inside it, shying away from the beaters again and again. They slowly move down the valley and finally stop in front of the prince and his entourage.

The stag stands there with trembling flanks. Foam drips from its mouth. It knows that there is no longer any point in trying to flee. That something is about to happen to it.

The prince, a heavy, dark man, hands a rifle to the princess. He is presenting her with the stag. She raises the rifle, takes aim, lets it drop. The hunting party surrounds her in a semicircle. The stag offers her its flank. She raises the rifle again. Again she lets it drop. The prince rips it from her hands then and shoots the stag. The princess turns around and runs to her coach.

Beaters gather up the kill and spread out long rows of dead animals. Horn players raise their instruments.

Tatlin goes over to the forester. With a smile, he offers him his silver flask. The forester takes a drink.

We're invited to the prince's hunting lodge, he says. In one hour.

She was the one who came up with the idea that Tatlin should precede her to America. As fragile as she appeared, she was driven by a formidable energy that was directed at Tatlin. He did her bidding; at the same time, he pitied her, wanted to protect her. Naturally, he didn't take seriously her totally insane fantasies about their future life in America. But neither did he contradict her. He had lost all distance to her. He let her rage within him as she wished.

Sometimes the letters that he wrote to her from his rooming house in the Bronx seemed to him to have been written by a stranger. What was this whole thing really all about? The intervals between her letters in reply got longer and longer, and the letters themselves got shorter. Then they stopped coming altogether. He was overcome by a searing agony. Was she sick? Had something happened to her? It was as if something was compelling him. He went back.

Torches were burning in the courtyard of the hunting lodge; beaters were turning wild boars on spits over several fires; a keg of beer had been tapped; and the hunting lodge glowed brightly. Inside the hall: benches full of people. On the tables: serving dishes full of roasted game, baskets of bread, apples, grapes. And in between: steins of beer and bottles of crystal-clear vodka. A band of gypsies is playing music. A fire burns in the huge fireplace.

Waltz music for the nobility issues from the adjoining rooms. It is early as yet. The alcohol is just beginning to take effect. People are cheerful; for the time being at least, they are still conforming to a certain etiquette.

At half past nine, the prince and princess make their appearance in the hall. The princess is a very young woman; he is massive and has a certain dark bonhomie about him. Eventually, they reach the table where Tatlin and the forester are sitting. The forester leaps to his feet at once when the prince speaks to him. The prince affably acknowledges the organization and smooth proceedings of the hunt. The forester modestly deflects the praise, remarking that Tatlin was a great help to him and adding that Tatlin happens to master a skill that is exceptional in its perfection, namely, knife-throwing.

The prince's eyes light up.

Like in the circus?

Tatlin rises to his feet.

Just like in the circus, the forester says. Place someone up against that door there, and he'll frame them with his knives.

The prince raises an arm. The band stops playing.

We have an artiste among us, he calls out.

It starts to quiet down. People from the adjoining rooms crowd into the hall.

A man who can frame a person with his knives.

He clears a path across the hall to a high oaken door.

Who wants to volunteer?

Tatlin looks at the princess. He looks her right in the eye. That is forbidden.

Who wants to volunteer? the prince calls out once again. Nobody? Am I surrounded by cowards?

It is suddenly silent in the hall. No one stirs. The prince looks ridiculous. Nobody is obeying him. And then the princess dashes through the open path. She bounces against the door, turns around. Tatlin takes his place opposite her. The prince really should go over to her and lead her out at this point. Tatlin waits.

Once he had returned from America, he went immediately to her parents' villa. He waited until one of the servants, an older woman, left the house. He spoke to her, made his inquiries. According to the woman, no one knew where the young mistress was. He got the same answer from the coachman. It was then that he took on his job as recruiter. That way, he could look for her.

The prince doesn't make any move whatsoever. The princess and Tatlin look at each other. Her eyes are wide open. A lady makes her way through the onlookers. She wants to take the place of the princess. The prince waves her off.

Tatlin and the princess look at each other. Slowly, Tatlin reaches into the inside pocket of his coat. With a lightning-quick movement, he hurls the knife. It flies past her right ear into the wood, quivers a little, then it is motionless.

A murmuring pulsates through the crowd.

Once again, Tatlin reaches for a knife. He holds it between his fingertips; suddenly, he throws it. It flies past her left ear and lodges with a dry plunk in the door.

Breathless silence. That can't possibly go well a third time. The prince doesn't move.

Tatlin draws the third knife.

This is the last one, he says.

A woman begins to sob.

What's happening here is a sin, someone calls out.

The prince flings an arm into the air.

Silence! he shouts.

They look at each other. The palms of her hands are facing outward, toward him. Tatlin throws the knife.

It flies right over her hair into the wood.

An outcry ripples through the hall. The princess rushes out. Tatlin goes over to the door and removes his knives from the wood. The band starts to play again. He pushes his way through the crowd. He hears the applause and shouting behind him. It does him good to be in the darkness, and in the silence, and with the horses.

In the end, he had managed to locate her after all. She was walking across the marketplace in Kraków. On the arm of a man. The man was his best friend.

4

The bacillus and the bottom line

*Simon Kantor sees a diamond and shaves off his
beard. The Orient Express.*

Remedies for cholera: a warm, two-percent tannic
acid solution administered repeatedly in half-gallon doses;
purgatives (chlorine water, lactic acid, bismuth, calomel, iodine,
quinine, creosote, hydrochloric acid, strychnine, arsenic); baths
in water heated up to 96.8 ° F; opium; embrocations of ammo-
nium; bloodletting; Spanish fly; leeches; intravenous infusions
of saline solution.

Every doctor treats it in a different way. Albert Werth cannot
discern any type of system to it. There is apparently no method
of treatment that could be said to be successful. He begins to
suspect that the mortality rate (roughly 50 percent) is the same
with or without treatment. A feeling of powerlessness, and of
apathy, begins to spread within him. He looks at someone who
is dying without emotion. All he feels is a weariness so great
that he thinks he will never recover from it.

The epidemic sputters out in the middle of November.
Approximately ten thousand people are dead. Albert Werth
returns home to his parents and goes to bed.

Although the epidemic is over, the Hamburg senate extends
the prohibition on transporting Russian passengers even further. Not only steerage passengers are no longer allowed to be
transported, but also the few who have tickets for the expensive
second cabin class. That means that HAPAG has lost this source
of income as well. Their business of transporting emigrants has
reached rock bottom. But that was HAPAG's most important
source of income. Albert Ballin, the head of HAPAG, will have
to think of something.

Eydtkuhnen is teeming with emigrants who have HAPAG tickets. With a bit of luck, Simon Kantor was able to rent a room in the cottage of an old woman. He sits there now and tries to calculate how far he can get on the money he has left. Naturally, this Ehrlicher chap paid him far too little for his house. After the money for the tickets was subtracted, there was practically nothing left over. Simon Kantor keeps calculating. He doesn't give a hoot about that Eydtkuhnen out there. He doesn't even want to see it.

Ruth and Daniel feel differently. They are curious. And besides, the room is very small, and Simon is in a bad mood.

Ruth Kantor is a guileless person. She harbors no ulterior motives. Yet something must have been at work inside her, something along the lines of an analytical operation. For on the third day, while she was walking through Eydtkuhnen holding Daniel's hand, she asked an imposing gentleman for the time. There was a thick, golden watch chain displayed upon his not inconsiderable belly.

The man, flattered and eager to oblige, pulled out the watch that hung on the chain and flipped open the cap, only to discover with annoyance that it was slow again. In fact, it had stopped.

Daniel grasped the significance of the situation at once. If you're looking for a watchmaker, he peeped, my papa lives around the corner there in the widow Lang's house. And thus Simon Kantor acquired his first customer in Eydtkuhnen.

It was only then that it dawned on Ruth what an ingenious idea she's had. From that time onwards, she walked incessantly through Eydtkuhnen with Daniel, asking gentlemen for the time. It was incredible how many watches didn't work and were carried around just the same. Due to this contradiction in which they were caught out, the gentlemen, put to shame like that, were then quite prepared to have Simon Kantor repair their watches. It was practically a point of honor, and soon Simon Kantor had plenty to do.

Dr. Albert Werth sleeps. He sleeps for one night and one day and one night.

44

Nobody can sleep that long, says his father, the lawyer Werth.

They can, too, when they've been through what he has, answers his wife.

You'd think he would get hungry, says the lawyer Werth.

I'll go over to him right away, says his wife.

Albert, she breathes. Are you asleep?

Yes, Albert growls.

Don't you at least want some breakfast?

I want to be left in peace.

But a little later, she tiptoes into the room carrying a tray with breakfast arranged on it. She puts it on a chair next to the bed and tiptoes back out. Half an hour later, she peeks through the keyhole. The entire contents of the tray have been eaten. She reports this to her husband that evening.

Then he's survived, says the lawyer Werth, and marches into his son's room. His wife remains in the parlor. She can imagine what will come next. She hears the overly cheerful voice of her husband. Then it becomes quieter and takes on a pleading tone. Suddenly, a shout: Albert, I'm talking to you! A pause. The lawyer Werth stomps back into the parlor. He is sweating. Exhausted, he falls into an armchair.

He won't speak.

Well, then he's just not speaking, says his wife.

But the next morning, Albert Werth speaks.

Mama, he calls out.

She is at his side at once.

Albert.

It stinks here, says Albert.

It stinks here, does it? his mother cries indignantly. That can't possibly be — two fanlights are open.

It stinks, says Albert. You've got some eau de Cologne, perfume. I have to do something about this stench.

She brings him everything she has.

In the evening, when he hears that his son still hasn't got up, the lawyer Werth decides to have another go at it. He comes back greatly upset.

It stinks in there like a seven-story cathouse, he exclaims.

Richard! his wife cries in outrage.

Maybe we should call a doctor, the lawyer Werth says.

He *is* a doctor, his wife replies.

Albert Werth lies shrouded in a thick cloud of perfume. But it stinks nonetheless. It stinks of hospital. Of shit and of Lysol. He knows that there's something wrong with him. That's because there is something else entirely that's wrong with him. Something that always used to happen whenever he went to bed, or slept, or woke up didn't happen anymore. In the hospital, he didn't have time to think about that at all. But now he did have time to think about it, and he does think about it, but still nothing happens. He's dead down there.

He tries to help matters along. Nothing. He looks at volumes of artwork. *Venus of Urbino. Sacred and Profane Love.* Nothing. He knows that there is an envelope with some photos hidden behind certain books. He hasn't looked at them since his secondary-school days. He rummages around and pulls them out. Nothing. He reviews the daydreams he used to have, the ones that always recurred. That he is fourteen, for instance, and his Aunt Lissy takes him to Travemünde with her. Just the two of them. They have connecting rooms. She bathes him. At night, he slips into her bed. Her scent.

Nothing. Lifeless straw. And he can't sleep anymore either. Thus, he does not put up any resistance when his father makes him a proposition.

That morning, the lawyer Werth had gone to the post office located on Schlüterstraße, where he had them send a long telegram. The answer arrived that evening.

Uncle Papo has invited you to Damascus, father Werth says, and waved the telegram.

Simon Kantor, then, has work to do once again, and the more work that comes his way, the more interested he becomes in that Eydtkuhnen out there. Sometimes he takes a break and wanders around the city. He is overwhelmed. For the first time in his life, he sees tall houses. Three stories. It's mind-boggling. And paved streets. And shops.

46

Couldn't we go back? Ruth says. Nothing has happened after all.

Where your best friend was practically about to kill you, that's where you want to return to?

When will they ever get it?

We refused to admit it, but we were always foreign to them; we're still in exile. And the laws that the czar passed only reinforced them in that belief. Without those laws, things might have remained without incident.

But we could stay here, in Eydtkuhnen.

That was indeed worthier of consideration.

He had unpacked his kitchen timers, had put together his wall clocks again, and displayed the jewelry on a little table. And one or the other of his customers who had him repair their watches also would buy a timer; or they came back because they had decided to buy a wall clock, or a ring for the wife. Little by little, word got around that there was a clockmaker in town, and a cheap and good one at that. Simon Kantor was summoned to people's houses. Grandfather clocks, mantelpiece clocks, wall clocks, pendulum clocks, musical clocks — clocks all over the place that refused to work; that chimed incorrectly or not at all; that were too fast or too slow; that were rusty; or whose works had seized up due to lack of proper oiling.

If he had been overwhelmed by Eydtkuhnen's streets, this was nothing compared to how he felt when he entered the interiors of certain homes, such as the living room of the railway inspector Bein, the dining room of the timber merchant Meier, or the parlor of the district administrator, Mrs. Böhlich. He hadn't thought such luxury, such opulence, such taste possible. All these wall cupboards; table and chair legs overgrown with wooden clusters of grapes and blossoms; these puttos and caryatids made of oak and walnut; the bronze lions' heads; not to mention these incredibly exquisite crocheted doilies and antimacassars on little side tables and armchairs; or these bloodred Persian carpets and runners.

No, this Eydtkuhnen could have captivated Simon Kantor, no doubt about it; he was even supposed to repair the clock in the church tower. But from a certain afternoon on, there was no more talk of staying. On that afternoon, Simon Kantor saw his first diamond.

A matter of not a little significance was *where* he had seen it. He had seen it in the parlor of the district administrator, Mrs. Böhlich; to be more precise, in her décolleté.

Now, the district administrator's décolleté happened to be famous in the city of Eydtkuhnen; therefore, the district administrator was by no means surprised that this young man was staring at her. Nevertheless, she said: What are you staring at like that?

Which left Simon Kantor in something of a bind. If he had said, I'm staring at the diamond, that would have been an insult. If he had said, I'm staring at your bosom, it would have been one as well. He got out of this delicate situation by stammering: I've never seen anything so beautiful before.

The district administrator took that to mean her bosom, and blushed in an accomplished manner.

One doesn't say such things, young man, she said. One merely thinks them. And now you will repair the pendulums.

Despite the fact that the diamond he had seen was small (he will realize only later on how small it actually was), it had kindled a fire in him just the same — a cold fire glowing blue-white. Simon Kantor now wanted to go to America. He wanted to go to America no matter what.

When Ruth and Daniel returned home, something had happened. They stared at him aghast. Simon Kantor had shaved off his beard.

Did they know this man? Yes, they did know him. But they didn't know that he had such a finely molded, narrow face; such handsomely — and bewilderingly so — curving lips; or such a resolute chin.

Ruth blushed. She was confused. An Orthodox Jew didn't do what he had done. She was ashamed for him. And because of that, she didn't ask him why he had done it. Simon Kantor was secretly grateful to her for that. How could he have told her about the diamond without telling her where he had seen it, in which dizzyingly deep, creamily soft white chasm; and what that had to do with the fact that he had shaved off his beard, and with America?

Upon beholding that diamond, he had felt something that couldn't be described by words like wrath or fury, although it had something to do with wrath and fury. It was something cold, something coldly gleaming like that stone. Nobody would be able to make him run away anymore, he suddenly thought. No longer would he have to be ashamed of his earlier humiliation.

Ruth looked at him. He was sitting at the table, bent over a watch, with his magnifying glass wedged into one eye. He radiated an energy that wasn't present in him before. She felt compelled to look over at him again and again. She did it against her will, and with a guilty conscience. But something forced her, and that something was sin. Because it was all connected to the fact that he had shaved his beard. That his face was naked. His naked face aroused her.

But she was a respectable woman! What she now couldn't stop thinking about had, in the past, always taken place in the dark, under the covers, with eyes closed and motionless, as her duty and obligation. However, on the evening of the day when he had shown himself to her with his naked face, she lay next to him and, for the first time ever, waited for him to come to her; she hoped, she wanted him to come; she felt for the first time a heat between her legs that only he could ease, and only by her looking at his naked face while it took place. He must have sensed something, because he went to her that evening, and she did something that she had never done before, something that a respectable woman doesn't do. She had taken his hand and pressed it between her legs. And on that evening, she experienced something that she had never experienced before; it was such that he had to put his hand over her mouth.

This was no cause for rejoicing. Simon Kantor had turned into a man whom she no longer knew. That scared her. But inside her, too, something was unfolding; something that she hadn't known about herself, and this scared her as well. She wanted to kiss his face constantly. She forced herself not to look at him, or to look away when he spoke to her. But that did little to help her predicament. She could see his face with her eyes closed, too. He must have been able to sense something. He must have sensed the conscious effort it took for her not to look at him; the pain it caused her to act cold. But that very fact seemed to spur him on. Before, he would leave her alone when she resisted. Now, however, he smiled and persisted. She acted indifferent; she acted scandalized; but inside her something called out: Keep going, don't stop, come.

But were they not married? Still, one is not allowed to do it like that, she thought. It's a sin like that.

But maybe America was a country where one was allowed to do it. To do it like that. A country where it wasn't a sin.

Albert Werth boards the Orient Express in Munich. He knows what the Compagnie Internationale des Wagons-Lits et des Grands Express Européens, founded by the Belgian Georges Nagelmackers, is. He knows that this train, shimmering in sumptuous shades of blue and gold, is a legend. Yet he boards it with a sulky casualness, as if he's getting on a Hamburg streetcar. He doesn't permit himself to be impressed by the mighty black locomotive, and its huge red wheels, and the white clouds of steam that it belches; nor by his compartment with its rosewood paneling and the inlays in the shape of blossom sprays. He does, however, test his reclining seat, which the conductor will turn into a bed at night. He examines the sink with its warm- and cold-water faucets, and the cabinet fitted with mirrors, in which he discovers heavy glasses made of crystal and a carafe with water. He turns on and off the reading lamp above his bed, and the blue night-light, too, which shines in case the traveler has to get up during the night. Then he distributes his travel paraphernalia quickly and in a businesslike manner. He will have to spend the next four days in this carpet-padded, golden brown chamber.

No, it isn't that easy to make him feel cheerful. The dining car can't do the trick either; nor can all that silver and crystal set out on the damask tablecloths. They can cook, I'll give them that much, he does admit to himself upon returning to his compartment immediately following dinner. On his way back, he buys a copy of the *Times* at a newsstand. At this moment, he feels positively Hamburgian. Which is to say: thoroughly sober-minded and matter-of-fact, if you please.

Even the word Damascus fails to excite him. He doesn't care to where and to whom he is traveling. They had relatives in London and in Paris, but nobody knows this Uncle Papo, this spice merchant. He sends his congratulations to all the celebrations, but beyond that, he was a rumor, a joke, one who stood for something exotically Oriental. The only person who could have told them how he was related to them was Grandma Werth, had she still been alive. Actually, they should have called him Uncle Eli. But they called him by his last name, which, to the family members in Hamburg at least, sounded kind of like baby talk. In fact, Papo was a traditional Sephardic surname. They all came from Spain originally. When they were driven out of Spain, they emigrated to Portugal, and from there, either to the Orient or via Amsterdam to Hamburg.

Maybe it will be pleasant, he thinks.

He opens up the *Times* and loses himself in an article about the quality of English coals. He reads for a while; but then, his gaze becomes fixed.

What is that?

It's unbelievable; it can't be true. But it is true. Downright painfully true.

He lowers the newspaper. What he had tried to coax into happening with pictures and photographs had come to be for no particular reason. Or were the vibrations from the moving train the cause? Whatever the case may be, Albert Werth has a tremendous - what do they call it? — hard-on.

He puts the newspaper aside and gets up. He goes into the dining car. He must distract himself. He orders a bottle of red wine. This could turn out to be one fine night, he thinks. While making his way back to his compartment late that evening, he staggers more than a little.

As it turns out, all his worrying was for naught. When he lies in his bed at last, everything remains calm. In fact, he sleeps well. He sleeps downright delightfully. Borne through the night of a strange country, he lies surrounded by the soothing rhythm of the wheels turning, like he last had as an infant in swaddling clothes.

5

First hot, then cold

A nun on leave. Beware of small men.
Dr. Werth receives a fez.

A small, black cloud appears on the horizon, causing the group gathered in front of the wooden shed to break
into cheering and yelling. The servants Jacobus and Hendrik
begin to hop up and down, screeching at the same time. The
nurses Veronika and Martha start to sob. Father Martin
shouts: There it is. Off in the distance, where the tracks meet to
form a single silver dot, something black has appeared under
the cloud of smoke. It gradually becomes larger and they can
hear the far-off noise of the locomotive and the chugging of the
train. Sister Alma is now completely surrounded. Everyone,
with the exception of Father Martin of course, wants to be as
close to her as possible; to throng around her; to touch her. She
squeezes their hands, strokes heads and cheeks. There are tears
in her eyes, and she calls out repeatedly: But I'll be back soon
anyhow! A sign is nailed to the wooden shack. Painted black
on a white background is the word Karibib. Underneath that,
some wag has written Central Station.

The light-rail locomotive with its three open carriages emits
a triumphant whistle. Then it begins to brake. The train comes
to a halt, squealing and rumbling. Sister Alma makes her way
out of the circle that surrounds her and climbs onto the last
carriage that is protected from the sun by an awning. Jacobus
hands her the suitcase, Hendrik the deck chair. Everyone
reaches out for her with their hands now. The locomotive
whistles again and the train slowly begins to move. The servants
Hendrik and Jacobus run alongside it for a while, then they are
left behind; they wave like all the others in front of the wooden
shed, who grow smaller and smaller but continue to wave
doggedly. Only when the train has rounded a hill and the group
has disappeared does Sister Alma lower her arm and turn to

face the head wind. The air is fresh and cool; it is early in the morning and the sun hovers just above the horizon.

The countryside slowly glides by: semidesert, with a few thornbushes scattered between boulders. After a while, she opens the deck chair and takes a seat upon it; and thus, having settled into a position that is unusually laid-back for a nun, especially for a Dominican nun, she merrily bumps and bounces along on the route to Swakopmund.

Three days later, she is standing at the railing of the steamboat *Gertrude Woermann* from Hamburg. The steel planks vibrate beneath her feet. The ship's engines are running at full speed. The breakers, the few little houses on the shore, and the grayish brown desert landscape behind them are getting imperceptibly smaller, as if they are being pushed back against the horizon. She'll return in a little over three months. After five years of ministering to the sick at the missionary station in Karibib, she has been allowed to take a period of leave at her order's mother house.

Six weeks later, she sits in a house in Bad Kleinen, a town located on the Berlin – Hamburg railroad line. A letter had arrived for her at her mother house a week earlier. Help me, her aunt wrote. I am dying. Because her aunt had made her sole heiress, her superiors agreed to grant Sister Alma permission to go to her. They expected her to donate her inheritance to the order.

She tries to write a letter. She hasn't got beyond the date and the introductory greeting: Praised be Jesus Christ in all eternity, amen.

She gets up and goes into the room of the dying woman. Her mouth is open; her breathing is labored and makes a rattling sound. Sister Alma trickles water from a damp cloth onto the woman's cracked lips. She returns to the living room and sits down in front of the letter she has begun.

She looks at the wedding ring on her left hand.

You're married? the Hottentot (Khoikhoi) women had asked. Where is your husband?

I am a bride of Christ.

You're married to a god?

Engaged. There are no other gods before Him.

And where are your children?

I am engaged.

How many brides does your god have? So many?

They looked at each other in disbelief.

How often does your god come to you?

They asked in a serious and matter-of-fact manner. They were perfectly willing to try to understand.

The doorbell rings. Kupfer, the notary public, is bringing her the documents, ready to sign, as he puts it. He reads the will and shows her where she needs to sign, first the inheritance papers and then the sale contract — he already has someone who's interested in buying the house. The only thing missing now is the death certificate.

I'd like the money in cash, says Sister Alma. In hundred-mark bills.

She wanders through the house. She is now twenty-six. She entered the convent at the age of fourteen. She has only a dim memory of her parents, both of whom are dead; she has no memories at all of her siblings, all of whom are much older. She walks through the house as if she is walking through a museum. So this is how people live. This is how they cook; here is where they eat; here is where they sleep. Photos on the wall. Weddings, births, excursions, group pictures. Happy times.

She goes back downstairs and sits in front of the letter she has started.

When she went to sign the documents, she had to stop and think for a moment. Finally, she wrote Alma Laufer. Laufer was her civil name. To whom does it refer? Which person?

She goes over to her aunt. She stops in the doorway. It is quiet; only the ticking of the alarm clock on the bedside table can be heard. She takes it out of the room. She binds the dead woman's lower jaw with a strip of cloth so that her mouth is not gaping open. She fetches water and towels to wash her. She dresses her in a fresh nightgown and folds her hands on her breast. She closes the curtains and lights two candles, one on each side of her aunt's head. Now a corpse lies there.

She has no reason to be shaken. Not theologically speaking either. And she has seen so many die already.

The notary public Kupfer shows up right away on the following day. He takes a thick envelope from his pocket.

Please count it, he says. And sign the acknowledgment of receipt here. She hands him the death certificate in return. After he has left, she removes the money from the envelope — a thick wad of bills. She has never possessed any money up till now. She smells it.

Simon Kantor goes to the HAPAG agency from time to time. Mr. Ehrlicher throws his hands into the air whenever he appears. Still nothing new, he cries in despair. But people who have booked a passage via Bremen are allowed to cross, Simon Kantor says.

As if the germ could tell the difference between Hamburg and Bremen.

At least as desperate as Ehrlicher is his boss, the head of HAPAG's passenger-ship division, Albert Ballin. Over the past few years, HAPAG had realized an annual profit of ten million marks with its emigrant business alone. That this should now come to an end is simply unacceptable.

Ballin does what he always has done — he negotiates. To be exact, he negotiates with HAPAG's fiercest competitor, the shipping company Bremer Lloyd. Ballin is a very small man. At the young age of eighteen, he had attained the power to act and sign on behalf of his father's emigration agency (he had to be declared of full legal age prematurely for that very purpose); he had wheeled and dealed his way to the top of the passenger-ship division at HAPAG, right onto the board of directors. He has made the balancing of everyone's interests his principle. The pie is big enough for everybody to get their piece of it, and so they should. The energy with which he compels his rivals to cooperate appears to be connected to his small size. He is not a handsome man either. He was forced to consider what kind of impression he made on others at an early age. Which means that he has some grasp of psychology. Moreover, the shippers of emigrants do not enjoy a very good reputation in Hamburg, especially when one of them is poor and Jewish like Ballin. The emigrant business has a whiff of the slave trade about it. For him, power has a different taste to it than it does for patricians' sons like Laisz or Mönckeberg or Sloman — an acrid taste.

He rings for his secretary. He has an appointment with the mayor. He has managed to convince the gentlemen of Bremer Lloyd that the closing of the imperial borders could not possibly be in their best interest either. He has talked them into writing a joint letter to the Prussian Minister of the Interior. He intends to inform the mayor about the contents of that letter. In addition, he wants to present the senate with a gift.

That gift rests on top of his office's conference table that is covered with green Morocco leather; it is a shallow chest painted green, roughly two yards long and one and a half yards wide. Handles have been attached to its corners.

Ballin's secretary helps him into his coat; two employees lift the wooden chest off the table; and the secretary tucks a large black roll of cardboard under his own arm. This is how they set out for city hall.

In addition to Mayor Mönckeberg, Senators Versmann and Hachmann are present when Ballin is admitted. He informs these gentlemen that HAPAG and Bremer Lloyd have appealed to Prussia's Minister of the Interior in a joint letter. He reports at length about how difficult the negotiations were, but also how they came to realize that they share a common interest. He wants these three men to comprehend, really comprehend, the significance of the fact that two of Germany's largest shipping companies have joined forces on this matter. He still hasn't said a word about the chest out in the antechamber.

In the letter, says Ballin, we have calculated for Prussia's Minister of the Interior that the closing of the border will mean more than two million marks' worth of shortfall in receipts for the Prussian railroad, and it will cost the steamship lines between eight and nine million marks.

The gentlemen look very distressed. They know what that amounts to in terms of loss of tax revenue.

Now Ballin plays his trump card. But if the reason for the

blockade is a fear that epidemics will be imported, he says, this could be allayed by erecting control stations at the border to examine the emigrants for diseases.

The gentlemen look doubtful. All three are thinking the same thing: And who's supposed to pay for that? We, perhaps?

Ballin paused. Then he says: The stations would be built and run at the expense of HAPAG and Bremer Lloyd.

Their smiles signal relief, but also appreciation.

Naturally, the opening of Hamburg's state borders would be a prerequisite, says Ballin. The gentlemen become serious again, but remain calm and composed. They could always hide behind Prussia's Minister of the Interior if need be.

And now for a more pleasant topic, Ballin exclaims. He's brought something for the senate. That something is in the antechamber. Amused, they rise to their feet. The gentlemen stand in front of the green chest, not knowing what to make of it.

This, exclaims Ballin while folding back the lid with a flourish (not unlike a circus director), is a model. The model of a small city.

The gentlemen come closer.

The conditions in the emigrants' huts located at the America quay are scandalous, says Ballin, and not just since the cholera epidemic.

Ballin's secretary lifts up the roof of one of the long buildings. Their curiosity piqued, the gentlemen bend over it. How darling, says Mönckeberg. One tiny bed after the other lines up to form two long rows.

We must look to the future, says Ballin.

Versmann lifts the roof of a smaller, almost square building. A church, a Protestant one. Hachmann discovers a Catholic one; Mönckeberg a Jewish prayer hall. Regular little benches and chairs, all true to scale. Giggling, the gentlemen point out details to each other.

The streams of emigrants are going to swell, says Ballin. It is in Hamburg's interest as well that they be provided shelter that is fit for human beings.

Versmann has discovered the kitchen with its chopping blocks, kettles, and cute little pots and pans. Delightful.

They're not listening to me, thinks Ballin. I might as well have given them a dollhouse.

Mönckeberg has found the room with the steam engines that are to provide electricity; Hachmann has located the music pavilion.

This facility will be able to house five thousand people, says Ballin, a little city in and of itself. It will be the most modern and comfortable accomodation for emigrants in all of Europe. HAPAG would expend a million marks on it. Provided...

The gentlemen straighten up.

Provided, says Ballin, that Hamburg make available the building ground for the project in Veddel, in the southeast of the city.

The gentlemen look at him.

I see, says Hachmann.

We'll think about it, says Mönckeberg.

I'll leave the model and the plans here with you, says Ballin. Good day.

Two senate clerks gaze after Ballin as he leaves city hall with his secretary.

In the old days, they'd have called someone like him a slave trader.

But isn't he helping the Russian Jews escape persecution?

Hypocrite. All he cares about is the money.

But isn't what I just said true?

That's so typical of a Jew. Money and morality.

What does that have to do with the fact that he's Jewish? Any other man at the head of HAPAG would do what he's doing; they'd have to. Because of exactly the same anti-Semitism that you're exhibiting right here and now, the Jews have to flee Russia.

And so Prussia's Minister of the Interior reviews Ballin's suggestion, and the Hamburg senate does so as well. Yet one morning, Ballin blows his top. He dictates a letter. He arranges another appointment with Mayor Mönckeberg. He storms into city hall. The senate is more than happy to take in tax revenue from HAPAG, he hisses. But what does Hamburg do for

HAPAG in return? I also should like to inform you that I have just written a letter to the chamber of commerce. If Hamburg does not open its borders to Russian emigrants, HAPAG will have no choice but to transfer its headquarters to Nordenham near Bremerhaven. Good day, sir.

HAPAG has bought a plot of land, Ehrlicher calls out to Simon Kantor when the latter drops in again. Something is up. Two weeks after Ballin's little scene in city hall, the senate re-opened Hamburg's state borders to Russian emigrants. Prussia's Minister of the Interior, however, continues to review the matter.

Sister Alma still hasn't sent off the letter to her Mother Superior. She asks herself what she is waiting for. And it becomes clear to her that this letter, if not an act of outright disobedience, is nevertheless high-handed. She wants to decide for herself when she will return. She is confronting her Mother Superior with a fait accompli. When the letter from her aunt had arrived, Sister Alma had experienced an overwhelming sense of relief. But were things so wonderful in the scorching heat of Africa? she asked herself. Four little stone houses around a water hole, a couple of wooden sheds, and behind them, the huts of the Nama people, all set in a semidesert strewn with rocks, where only thornbushes grew, and here and there tufts of hard, tall grass — that's all there was. But there was the sky; there was the yellow glow when the sun went down behind the copper-colored mountains. There was the heat, and the frost; there were sandstorms and downpours of rain and clouds of stars. Don't change the subject, she thinks. Why this sense of relief? And it had been so intense that she had had a hard time keeping it to herself. Father Martin's written assessment of Sister Alma and her work had been so favorable that Mother Superior could not deny her request to visit her dying aunt, even though it was obvious that she would have liked to deny it. And suddenly, she knew why she had felt such relief when the letter arrived.

What exactly do the blacks eat anyhow?

Can they talk?

Do you really think they have a soul?

But then that would mean they're human beings.

Grown women, kept and treated as if they were half-wits.

Their narrow-mindedness, their lack of education, their malice. The envy, the scheming and intrigues. Is *that* any way to serve God?

Mother Superior pointedly had not asked her even a single question. That was comment enough.

She has grown hot. She accuses herself of being self-righteous, proud. Yet she senses that she is reproaching herself merely out of habit; and suddenly she asks herself what would happen when, in another five years, her time in Africa was up. She would return to her convent, what else? And all of a sudden, there is turmoil within her; panic; almost a scream.

No.

She leaps to her feet. She has to distract herself. She starts to pack. She soon has her own belongings together. Then she has an idea. She could do something to please the women in Karibib. She would bring them a couple of dresses. She goes upstairs to the bedroom. She pulls down a suitcase from the wardrobe. A red dress with a black pattern catches her eye; she likes this one a lot. It would look good on Mathilde. She goes over to the mirror and holds the dress in front of herself. And then she blushes. She is holding the dress as if she's checking to see whether it would look good on herself. She quickly tosses it into the suitcase.

Her hand bumps into something hard at the very back of a drawer: a small box. She opens it. Suddenly, it glitters. That is jewelry. She closes the lid again. She's not interested in that.

She goes downstairs. She sits in front of the letter again. Her aunt's funeral was three days ago. What is she doing here so long? I was permitted to be alone, she thinks. Nobody who wanted something from me; nobody who was watching me like a hawk. She was alone, all alone and to herself. It was a treat, the likes of which she had never experienced before; a voluptuous pleasure.

Suddenly, she folds the letter, puts it in the envelope, and goes out to the mailbox. She should have shorn her head again long ago.

Would you take a look at that, Mr. Ehrlicher calls to Simon Kantor. A wooden shed has been erected behind the HAPAG agency. They are in the process of installing windows. It can't be much longer now, says Mr. Ehrlicher.

Albert Werth sits on the roof terrace of Uncle Papo's house in Damascus with Uncle Papo, Aunt Rachel, and Cousin Louis. They've eaten roasted quail from a large silver platter. The housemaid brings the mocha. The evening sky over Damascus is made of pale blue enamel.

Uncle Papo speaks Arabic; Hebrew; Judezmo (also called Ladino), the Old Spanish of the Sephardic Jews; a little Italian; a little English; a little German. Louis is seventeen. He will take over his father's spice trade. He has pomaded his jet-black hair very thoroughly. He wears black oxfords with white leather trim. How old are you anyhow? he had asked the uptight German *Jeckes*. Twenty-six? he had exclaimed with disbelief in his voice.

Uncle Papo has given Albert Werth a red fez as a present. Louis decides to take charge of the further education of his cousin, and he decides to begin by introducing him to the night-life of Damascus. Dr. Albert Werth sits on Uncle Papo's roof terrace, a red fez on his head.

6

Travel acquaintances

What Prussian second lieutenants are made of.
Forged documents. How do the blacks talk?

Private First Class Groth stands next to the door at attention. He is wearing a uniform, jackboots, white gloves. A linen napkin is draped over the crook of his left arm. Seated at the table in the middle of the room, the second lieutenants von Reutersdorf, von Palen, von Tessenov, and Neuhaus have just finished dessert. PFC Groth sees the gentlemen, and then again, he doesn't see them. Second Lieutenant Neuhaus has made PFC Groth his orderly due to this ability to see things and not see them at the same time, among other reasons.

Groth gathers the crystal dessert dishes and spoons, then he goes into the kitchen and puts the water on. He carries demitasses and sugar over to the men. The second lieutenants are lighting their cigars. PFC Groth opens one of the window's fanlights. In the kitchen, he prepares the mocha coffee, carries it out to the dining room, and pours it; then he fetches the cognac decanter and snifters. After that, he withdraws to the kitchen.

Just as he has the ability to see something and not see it, he also is able to hear something, and then again, not hear it. He has heard how these gentlemen annexed Belgium's coal basin; how they occupied Paris; how they sank the British fleet; how they took the Ukraine; and how they founded colonies. He has heard all that, and then again, he hasn't. He has developed the ability to hear all that and still remain tranquil inside. Although usually coated with a thick gray layer of ice, sometimes there suddenly flares in him the desire to go out, get his carbine, and blow them all away as they sit there.

Any minute now, Second Lieutenant Neuhaus will call out: Let's have us a proper beer at last. And there he goes: A proper beer at last. PFC Groth takes the keg, carries it over, taps it, and begins to draw four mugs. Second Lieutenant Neuhaus can't wait to get his hands on his mug. In reality, he hates beer. At the Neuhaus villa in Essen, they drink wine. Mostly French wine, a bottle of the stuff going for a sum that would take Klaus Groth six months of schlepping sacks in Hamburg's port to earn. PFC Groth knows that because on evenings like this, after Second Lieutenant Neuhaus has thrown up for the last time and PFC Groth has peeled off Neuhaus's puke-covered uniform and put him to bed, his superior officer tends to get chummy with him.

PFC Groth fills two buckets with water. He puts them in the hall, next to the door to the lavatory. He places cleaning rags next to them. He goes to the gentlemen and empties ashtrays, fills beer mugs. While he is returning to the kitchen, Second Lieutenant von Tessenov gets up and moves toward the door to go to the lavatory. Naturally, Groth lets him go ahead. Von Tessenov stops and looks at him, which is to say: He looks up at him. PFC Groth puts the two ashtrays down on the table and stands at attention.

Express deepest recognition, von Tessenov crows.

Von Tessenov is blond, chubby, pink as a piglet, and over a head shorter than Groth.

Groth places his hands at his trouser seams, lightly clicks the heels of his boots together, and says: Most humble thanks, Second Lieutenant, sir! When von Tessenov returns, Groth goes into the lavatory and wipes Second Lieutenant von Tessenov's piss from the floor.

Second Lieutenant Neuhaus had ordered two plates of cold meats and other delicacies from Kempinski. His guests are from Mecklenburg and Brandenburg; their fathers grow potatoes or barley, and Second Lieutenant Neuhaus had to explain to them what was on the platters: truffles, breast of pheasant, morels, caviar. Second Lieutenant Neuhaus's invitations are much sought-after, although nobody would ever dream of admitting to that fact.

Groth hears how Neuhaus tries to imitate their awful Berlin dialect, and he hears how he talks on the phone to his mother in his Rhenish singsong. He says to himself: They've got a rolling mill with three thousand workers in Oberhausen, why does he put up with that from these Prussian starvelings?

It is, however, not a terribly urgent question for Groth. Some people have three thousand men toil away for them, and others thirty. What's the difference?

In the other room, things are getting boisterous. They're over in Africa with the Hottentot women.

Second Lieutenant Neuhaus's toilet paraphernalia are made of heavy silver. He loves mirrors and scents of all kinds. He wears silk nightshirts and reads books of poetry. For maneuvers, he has a set of toiletries that corresponds roughly to that of Second Lieutenant von Tessenov, and similar underwear as well. PFC Groth wonders how it is that Second Lieutenant Neuhaus is so sure he doesn't go around telling people everything he sees laid out on his superior officer's dressing table. Neuhaus would be the laughingstock of the regiment if he did.

Sometimes, when his guests have gone home after one of these so-called gentlemen's evenings, and Neuhaus has thrown up for the last time and hangs limply over the toilet bowl, Groth simply picks him up and carries him to bed. On these occasions, Groth feels sorry for him. He has so much money. Why is it so important to him to serve in this of all regiments? On parting, Neuhaus had asked him if he didn't want to stay on and become a professional soldier. When Groth smiled and shook his head, Neuhaus slipped him a hundred-mark bill and said: Thank you.

Groth is sitting in an express train that is traveling from Berlin to Hamburg. Sitting across from him is a married couple with a young boy. They are speaking Yiddish. After a while, the man addresses him in German: Is he is going to Hamburg as well? Groth then has to tell them about Hamburg.

Tatlin is sitting three rows away. He couldn't help smiling when he saw the little clockmaker. He recognized him at once. He was so afraid when he sold him, that is, Mr. Ehrlicher, his house. Kantor has yet to spot him.

Just how lucky it was that he went outside and rode off after he had performed his knife-throwing feat for the prince became clear to him only much later, when he was already far away from the hunting lodge. If he had stayed just another fifteen minutes, which is how long it would have taken the prince to find out who he was, Rybakov would have had him detained at once and shot. As it turned out, however, Prince Rybakov, division general, had been made to look an utter fool: He had wined and dined the very man who stole his recruits.

Was it instinct that had propelled him outside; a sudden foreboding that he was in grave danger? He still felt dazed hours later; still spellbound by that woman, her eyes. She had been testing the prince. If she meant anything to him, he would have held her back. He did not. Had she wanted the knives to kill her for that very reason? If he had hit her, both of them would have died. Were they both toying with the same desire then?

It was logical that he went outside; he did not wish to have his memory of that moment besmirched. It wasn't until the next morning that it dawned on him what had happened. The general would do everything in his power to hunt him down. This meant that he could forget about his business of recruiting emigrants; to do that, he would have to show himself in public. And what about the business with deserters? That had had to be transacted in secret right from the start. Why shouldn't that work in the future as well? Every day that he remained a free man made an even bigger fool of General Rybakov. This danger electrified him; it was a type of addiction.

Everything hinged on Semjonov. He was the one who produced the phony passports. He owned a small print shop in back of a dilapidated apartment house. He printed calendars, calling cards, posters, announcements. On the side, he also made etchings and copperplate engravings, little pictures of saints that he colored by hand. His bed was in the same room that held his old rattly press and his typecases. He left his cave only to procure the bare essentials — a human oyster.

The first time Tatlin had visited him, he bought a couple little saint pictures; then he felt him out a bit more. A friend of his had lost his passport. Finally, Semjonov got it. He didn't say yes or no. I'll be back in a week, said Tatlin, and left him the money and a piece of paper with the data for a twenty-one-year-old. The passport that Semjonov gave him was of excellent quality, as was everything that Semjonov left for him in the drop they had set up.

He had to avoid cities and larger towns, and the main roads. He had the lines of communication with the recruits in the barracks go through as many middlemen as possible, all of whom were small farmers. Their hatred of the kulaks and the authorities guaranteed that they would never betray him. And of course he paid them, too. Tatlin first laid eyes on the deserters when he handed over the passports and was paid, and they were practically on the run already. He summoned them individually, and he described the meeting place in vague terms on purpose. But how is he supposed to find you there? he was asked. He won't find me, he then replied, I'll find him. He wanted to observe the man for a while at first, to make sure he was really alone.

However, it appeared that Rybakov was on to him and his tactics. One evening, he put up at an inn that he had considered safe up till then. He went through the taproom, through the door behind the bar, and up the stairs. Once upstairs, he stopped all of a sudden. The two men at the table in the far corner. He didn't have anything solid to go on, just the uneasy feeling that there was something fishy about them.

He cautiously entered his chamber, slipped through the window and onto the roof of the shed below, and jumped to the ground. He led his horse out of the stall and went down to the street with it. Then he saddled up and mounted. More and more often now, he had the feeling that there were people sitting in the inns and taverns who didn't belong there. Rybakov had begun to plug his paths of escape and his hideouts. And on the lesser, more remote roads, Tatlin began to encounter more and more riders with conspicuously well-fed horses, the likes of which no farmer would ever be able to afford. Yet Rybakov evidently did not want to take any risks. He wanted to maneuver Tatlin into a situation that left him no way out. And that situation had arrived.

He was surrounded. There were horsemen in front of him, behind him, in a semicircle around him, galloping toward him now — an entire cavalry unit. However, they hadn't surrounded him completely. There was a small opening. But it led through the pines, down an incline and into the swamp on the valley floor. He charged downhill, dismounted, and ran into the swamp. Although "run" is not the right word for the manner in which he moved forward. Grotesquely contorted, he leapt from one moss cushion to the next, as if the ground beneath him had become too hot. In fact, the moss cushions were able to bear his weight only for this brief period of time; had he stopped to rest on one, he would have sunk immediately. Splashing and twisting this way and that, he kept jumping onward until finally, he was able to throw himself into a willow shrub at the last second.

The riders had reached the edge of the moor; they dismounted. They laughed and called out to each other. Anyone who got themselves into that swamp did not come out again. But they wanted to wait a little while, just to be on the safe side. They lit a fire.

Tatlin heard them. He was hanging there in the willow, right above the water. A ringed snake swam up to him and looked at him. He saw those vertical pupils, that basilisk gaze, and he felt that Death was looking at him. And then he did something that was completely insane.

Bastards! he yelled at the men on the bank. You lick the boots they kick you in the face with.

It got quiet.

Bastards! he yelled again.

Still it was silent.

But then, a voice began calling out commands.

Ready, aim. Fire!

A volley of shots rained into the bush in which he hung.

Fire!

He was hit in the shoulder. And then he screamed. He didn't feel any pain yet. But he screamed just the same. He screamed as if he'd been shot in the stomach. At first, that was just cunning. Let them think he was done for. He screamed, and he was very well aware that he was acting. But he wasn't screaming from the safety of some stage. He was hanging there in this willow, not knowing when it would snap; he was hanging over this swamp that would swallow him up without a trace; and little by little, he started to forget about the soldiers who wanted to capture him.

Mama, he screamed.

Help me, Mama, he screamed.

God, he screamed. Where are you?

Finally, he was reduced to whimpering; then he fell silent. The riders extinguished the fire and mounted.

Simon Kantor wasn't so sure anymore that he wanted to go to America. He'd even been issued a trade license, and Ruth was right: Things in Eydtkuhnen weren't bad at all. But something about her had changed. Whenever the word America was mentioned, she no longer got all defensive, nor did she try to change the subject anymore. Now she was the one who wanted to talk about America. At first, she was very matter-of-fact — That can wait until we're in New York, or: We'll see about that when we're in New York — but then, she would talk about it for no reason at all. She started to describe it, to Daniel mostly. New York was a wide, green valley, crisscrossed by rivers that formed lakes everywhere, so that one was no longer sure whether the tracts of land were still connected to deeper earth and rock strata, or whether they weren't perhaps islands floating adrift on these incredibly clear, barely moving, sluggish waters that were iridescent in the warm humidity and in the sunlight, in which the distinction between water and land became blurred and the horizon and the heavens rounded to form a giant egg, shimmering like mother-of-pearl.

Once it became clear to Simon that Ruth was now the one who wanted to go to America, the diamond on the bosom of the district administrator began to grow larger again. It had become quite small; just a tiny sparkle, actually. But now it grew and grew until finally, it had taken on the proportions of a five-carat rock.

They had followed the construction of the control station with apprehension, although there was a diffuse kind of interest mixed in with the fear; and once they were done with the building and the first trains had departed, Simon Kantor said: Now. Ruth packed without protest.

They got through the dreaded medical examination, the shower, and the disinfection with no trouble at all. Dr. Menz waved them through; Simon Kantor had repaired two clocks for him. And so they stood there one cold, windy morning on the platform. The platform gradually began to fill; in the end, there were two or three hundred people who stood pressed close together. But this was not a normal crowd of people — nobody spoke; crying children were hushed. They had set out from somewhere deep in the heart of Russia; they had left behind their pitiful shacks, the grime-encrusted poverty, the desolateness of their villages. They couldn't go back anymore. Everything that was familiar, customary, and known lay behind them. But what was to come? They had heard the recruiters talk; they had heard the stories that they had sown among them. But those were words; words that seemed totally un-believable to them here and now, on this platform. They did not believe that they would ever get beyond this point here. A train would never come along to pick them up here.

But then, when one did come along, the doors flew open as if by magic, and there arose a deep, hoarse, terrific roar. They stormed the carriages, shouting like mad.

Simon Kantor didn't budge. No, he said. We are not going to submit ourselves to that. We'll take the regular train. It doesn't cost all that much more anyway. And by the way, he had sold all his clocks.

He managed to exchange their tickets for regular ones. That was the first success. In Berlin, they managed to get on the right train, and they got seats in one of the fourth-class compart-ments. It was harder for them to stand the sight of this monstrous wasteland of houses called Berlin, and to endure the feeling of terror it produced in them. It was only when the train passed through fields and forests and crossed little rivulets and streams that they looked at each other again. Finally, it was a success that they had struck up a conversation with this young man who was telling them about the city of Hamburg.

The train begins to brake. Houses appear; a station sign glides by — Bad Kleinen. The train grinds to a halt. The door is opened and two suitcases are shoved into the compartment. Everyone stares — a nun boards the train. She looks around for a seat and discovers one next to Simon Kantor. The young man from Hamburg and Simon Kantor heave her suitcases into the baggage net; she takes a seat.

Tatlin observes them for a while before going over to them. Simon Kantor is amazed.

Well, well, well. We meet again, Tatlin grins. May I join you? By then, he's already sitting next to Groth.

The nun looks at Tatlin. She looks at him, then looks away. For the duration of the journey to Hamburg, she does not look at Tatlin again.

Daniel is excited. She was in Africa, and that's where she's going back to? Are they really black down there? Can they speak? And what does it sound like?

They give a start. The nun is speaking. But she is speaking Nama, a soft, guttural sound, yet one that is interspersed with sharp clicks that cause them to jerk involuntarily. They stare at her.

And what does that mean? Daniel asks in confusion.

You are a handsome, intelligent boy and I like you, says Sister Alma.

They laugh, relieved.

And how do you say: The weather is fine and we are going to America? Daniel exclaims.

Again Sister Alma's lovely mouth makes cooing and clicking noises.

And how do you say: Once we're in America, we will soon be rich?

Daniel, that's enough now, Simon Kantor says.

They want Tatlin to tell them about America.

Tatlin rattles off the contents of the brochure that the recruiters have to learn by heart. He doesn't tell them what the Bowery is, or the Lower East Side. At some point, he stops talking. They look at him expectantly. And then he says: The Pilgrim Fathers came to America to build the heavenly Jerusalem, the city on the hill. Where swords are turned into plowshares and lances into vintners' billhooks. Each person will sit beneath his grapevine and his fig tree, and no one shall frighten him, because neither the blasphemers nor the liars nor the bearers of false witness shall enter. The entire city shall belong to the Lord. Tyrants will no longer dwell in the houses of God there; murderers will no longer be regarded as heroes, power and violence no longer holy.

Houses begin to appear outside. That's already part of Hamburg, says Groth. They leap to their feet and want to get into their coats.

Sit down, says Groth. We've still got a long way to go.

7

The treasure vault

Dr. Werth is back. Two jilted women. Belly dance.

A pungent yellow fog hangs over the city. It is damp
and cold. The chimneys of houses emit fumes; locomotives emit
fumes; and the smokestacks of ships and factories emit fumes.
Droplets of water condense on the soot particles in the air. It's
drizzling. Hamburg weather.

Albert Werth is walking along the street named Admirali-
tätsstraße, down to the port. He is headed for the warehouse
city, Speicherstadt, the mile-long reply to Bismarck's rape of
Hamburg; the brick overcompensation of the fear of joining the
Zollverein, the 19th-century customs union of German states;
the fortification, visible from afar, of that remainder of Hamburg's former glory which the Iron Chancellor let them keep —
the free port. A bulwark with stairwells, symbolically oversized
corner towers that would befit battlements, ecclesiastical point-
ed arches — an impressive stage setting whose reflection in the
water of the surrounding canals makes the glazed-tile-encrusted
façades appear even taller and more monumental than they are;
an enactment of power and prosperity; the architectural expres-
sion of the hopes and fears of Hamburg's *Pfeffersäcke*, as the
well-to-do spice merchants are somewhat derisively called.

Albert Werth dodges carts; he leaps over greenish yellow
puddles, over horse manure, and over a dead cat, too. At long
last, he is going to be permitted to enter the treasure vault that
he has seen only from the outside until now; this city within the
city, with its own post office, its own police station, its own fire
department, its own water and energy supply; the city of work
in which no one is allowed to live and from which even the
money-changers have been driven — the abridged version of
Hamburg.

The cargoes carried up the Elbe by the endless procession of
steamships are hoisted up from barges here, warehoused,

weighed, counted, assessed, packaged, and then lowered again onto carts and barges; the goods disappear into freight cars and are distributed throughout the country and across the border, to Poland, Russia, Austria, Hungary, and beyond. An entire section of the city was torn down and 24,000 people were thrown out of their homes (and nobody much cared where they were supposed to go afterwards) so that, in just over five years, the then biggest warehouse complex in the world could be erected — the worthy receptacle for the treasures of this earth and their transubstantiation into merchandise.

Albert Werth is approaching the two entrance towers of Brooksbrücke, one of the bridges leading into the warehouse city. Here, too, Hanoverian brick Gothic reigns supreme. The towers receive the visitor; they mediate between the secular world of the city outside and the sacred realm of the commercial holy objects within. It stinks. The stench comes from the harbor water, from the street, from everywhere. This was the breeding ground for cholera.

Visitors must be on their toes in order to dodge the carts, the carriers, the pallets of sacks and crates that are winched up or down from above. Woe to the person standing below if one of those sacks or crates falls down from the stacks up there. Whinnying of horses and shouting everywhere. The refined gentleman Dr. Werth is jostled more than once. Muffled tooting of the steamships; seagulls' cries; blows on iron ringing out from the Blohm & Voss shipyard; the pounding of steam-operated pile drivers.

Finally, a sign:

G. Voss & Cons.

4th Loft

He ascends the stairs, knocks on a door, and enters another world. He has been transported from Hamburg's yellowish gray gloom to a vault glowing in shades of brownish gold; from the stinking hell of the port to a heaven of aromatic delights.

Cardamom, turmeric, cumin, and saffron. Sumac, mastic gum, coriander, cinnamon. Ginger, paprika, aniseed, fennel, caraway, cayenne pepper. Nuts, seeds, dried fruit and pepper pods.

73

Voss and Consorts. Spices, retail and wholesale.

Vanilla as extract and in sticks, ground cinnammon and cinnamon bark, rosemary, cloves, thyme, nutmeg, and coffee and tea.

Mr. Voss delivers to bakeries, hotels, restaurants, railroad companies, cafés, makers of soft drinks.

I'm to give you kind regards from my uncle Eli Papo in Damascus, and the mail as well, says Albert Werth, pulling a pack of letters from his coat pocket.

Mr. Voss pours them each a glass of raki. He and Uncle Papo have been business partners for twenty years.

Sahtak, says Mr. Voss, and raises his glass. Albert Werth takes a sip and leans back, inhaling deeply.

This is how it smelled at Uncle Papo's, too.

A café violinist and a pianist; red carpets and velvet-covered chairs; marble and heavy china; the clinking of silver coffee and tea spoons; the sobbing of the violin — a café on Jungfernstieg, Hamburg's swank shopping avenue located next to the Binnenalster lake. A woman and a man enter. The woman is getting on in years; the man is young, very young. Not that he could be her son; her nephew is more likely, which would mean that she is his aunt. Yet a nephew would never behave like that with his aunt, thinks headwaiter Wintrich, and the aunt wouldn't laugh quite so loudly whenever the young man says something, and she wouldn't look at him like that. So enraptured.

On parting, Mr. Voss takes Albert Werth through the three rooms that are connected to his office. Clerks sit hunched over their orders, invoices, and letters. A spiral staircase leads down into a hall where they do the filling, weighing, packaging, and addressing.

Isn't there a chamber somewhere I could rent from you? says Albert Werth. Just so I could come here and sniff every once in a while?

He steps outside into the drizzle. Dusk is falling. The gaslights are already burning. He has to hurry. He still needs to change clothes before dinner. And he hasn't called Betty yet either.

The very young man in the café on Jungfernstieg leans over to his lady companion and whispers something in her ear. She bursts into laughter and gives him a pat on the cheek. He stands up and disappears in the direction of the lavatories.

Albert Werth looks at the table that has been set in the dining room of his parents — the damask tablecloth, the china, the crystal — and heaves a sigh of dismay. He is back in Hamburg. He greets the arriving guests. They heartily shake his hand. After all, his parents are hosting this dinner party to celebrate his return. But that is not the only significance of this evening's gathering. Above all Albert Werth's mother wants him to request Betty's father to step into one of the adjoining rooms when the gentlemen have withdrawn after dinner for mocha and cigars and, once there, to ask for his daughter's hand in marriage.

Damascus: a sand-colored maze of cubes, and towering above — minarets and the domes of the mosques, the gates of the citadel and Al-Azm Palace.

Albert Werth looks at Betty, pouting Betty — a splendid catch who would guarantee him an equally splendid future as Hamburg's leading fashionable doctor.

The dancer swirls from the wings onto the stage, a spiral made of red and blue veils. With an abrupt movement in the opposite direction, the veils come to a halt in the air; they float downward over an ample bosom, which is restrained only by an embroidered bandeau, and over a provocatively protruding white belly, upon which another embroidered sash disappears between her thighs.

The orchestra stops playing; a drum begins to beat a monotonous rhythm. The dancer stands still. Slowly, she begins to wriggle to the rhythm of the drum. It appears that she wants to avoid, to flee from something, yet something is also holding her in place; something that prevents her from moving her feet, but something that also fills her with pleasure the more she wriggles and the faster the drum beats.

She stops all of a sudden. She stands there as if chastised. But then, without the rest of her moving at all, her breasts begin to quake. Their slack fullness starts to come alive, as if they had a life of their own, and now her shoulders get into the act, too. She shakes her bosom, revealing its entire dimensions for the first time. The drum resumes, abruptly and brutally. Its rhythm gets into her pelvis, which begins to twitch back and forth, suggestively at first; then, however, with growing abandon and brazenness.

Again the drum stops. Again she stands still. And now the muscles of her belly begin to vibrate. Beads of sweat trickle down between her breasts. Her belly starts to undulate; an independent, alien being at this point. And then she collapses with a cry; she falls forward between her open legs, now just a billow of black hair and rounded back.

The young man in the café on Jungfernstieg would have been in the lavatory for half an hour now, had he gone to the lavatory. Headwaiter Wintrich decides to take a look. Just for the sake of order. He comes back and goes over to the table where the lady is sitting.

Can I get you anything else?

Another coffee please.

Mrs. Werth rises from table. The men retire to the smoking room. They return after half an hour. With pensive expressions on their faces. Everyone knew deep down that there was more to the purpose of this evening than welcoming home the Werth's son. They had prepared themselves for champagne and congratulations. But something had happened, and that something consisted in the fact that nothing had happened. Albert Werth did not ask Betty's father to step into the adjoining room. He had sipped his mocha and smoked his cigar.

And so the men returned to the parlor with sheepish looks on their faces, and the women knew what had happened without anyone having to say a word.

76

They chatted all the more cheerfully. They made conversation in a downright hectic manner. Luckily, they had Wormser. Daniel Wormser is a teacher at the Talmud-Torah Secondary School, a member of the German Central Committee for the Russian Jews, and founder of the Jewish Relief Society for the Homeless. As everyone feared he would, Wormser begins to talk about his charitable work. They gladly contribute, but they don't want to hear too much about all those Russian brothers and sisters in faith. With their lack of education and their unenlightened Ashkenazic fundamentalism, they are more or less an embarrassment to all these doctors, attorneys, bankers, and entrepreneurs. They don't want to be lumped together with them.

In the meantime, the lady is the only patron left in the café on Jungfernstieg. Headwaiter Wintrich goes over to her. I'm sorry, he says. But we're closing now.

They'd listened to Wormser; after fulfilling their obligation of politeness, however, they get ready to depart. At an unusually early hour, and all at once — almost as if they were taking flight.

Albert Werth says goodbye to his guests at the door. He says goodbye to Betty's parents; he says goodbye to Betty as well. He bows. They do not shake hands though.

What are you up to these days anyhow? Wormser asks him as they are taking leave of each other at the door. Why don't you stop by our relief society? We need doctors, says Wormser.

The coachman holds open the carriage door for Betty's parents. They get in. Betty climbs in behind them. She sits across from her parents, facing the back of the coach. After a while, her mother says: Betty.

Betty remains silent.

Betty, she says again.

Her husband places his hand on her arm. She dabs her eyes with a handkerchief.

Betty stares straight ahead, right through the space between them.

Albert Werth is well aware that the evening is not yet over. His mother intercepts him in the middle of the parlor.

I demand an explanation, she hisses.

I won't let myself be married off, he replies.

You never seemed to mind that up till now, she shouts.

But now I do mind.

What have you got against Betty?

Nothing, he says, just that I don't want to marry her, no matter how much money she has.

He leaves his mother standing there and goes to his room. He is back in Hamburg. Now the distorted cholera faces are returning.

He used to be such a nice student. But that was a long time ago; so long ago, it's as if it never was.

8

Chocolate

No limping allowed. Here's looking at you. Tears.

Dr. Werth descends a staircase. He hears the desk clerk say: You're in luck. Here he comes now. A nun addresses him.

An abscess in number sixteen, says the nun. Would he mind having a look?

Dr. Werth looks at the nun. He most definitely does not have time for that.

All right, he says. But it'll have to be quick.

The abscess is located on the outer left thigh; a huge boil.

A splintery piece of wood fell from the carriage and struck her leg, the woman relates. It bled some, and then the wound closed.

There's still something in there, the nun says.

Dr. Werth looks at her. Are you in the field?

Sort of, replies the nun.

The tiny chamber that they call room number sixteen here, in which two adults and one child are residing, would be called a broom closet in the lawyer Werth's house.

Tomorrow afternoon at four, says Dr. Werth. The nun smiles. He reaches for the door handle, misses it, then finally grabs hold of it. He smiles in return and walks out.

They had been very fortunate to meet this young man from Hamburg on the train. After they'd gone just the first few steps on the platform, he had said to Ruth: But you're limping.

There's something wrong with my leg. It hurts all the way down in my knee, too.

You'll never be able to get up the stairs at Ellis Island with that, the young man had replied. There's a wide staircase there, and everyone has to climb the stairs so they can see who's limping or panting or who has to stop. Anyone who hobbles gets a label with the letter L on it, for limping. And anyone who has that label attached to them gets sent back.

The young man was a blessing in general. Without him, they probably would have been cleaned out half an hour after their arrival, confused and scared as they would have been on their own, had they been talked into buying supposedly unbelievably cheap tinware, inexpensive quilts, and cleverly constructed spirit cookers. That's because the *Litzer*, which is what the bloodsuckers were called, fell upon the emigrants like a swarm of locusts, right there on the platform. As it turned out, the young man had warned them, even forbid them, to buy anything from these people, because for everything they would need on board the ship, there were price lists and addresses of shops where they could get the wares for a fraction of the price. And finally, he had taken them to a hotel; he even had haggled over the room price with the desk clerk in some strange-sounding tongue that was supposed to be German nevertheless. This meant that their accomodations for the period until they had to go into quarantine in the emigrants' huts on the America quay were, all things considered, fairly decent. The Kantors were in the aforementioned broom closet; Tatlin was in a dormitory with ten beds; and Sister Alma was in a double room.

And yet, that which they held to be a hotel didn't even call itself that. *Zum großen Auswanderer-Haus*, Big Emigrants' House, is what the yards-high letters proclaimed — a bleak, four-story box, a storage shed (but one for people): badly worn from their shoes and hands; caked with their dirt; falling apart and full of lice; a palace for cockroaches and rats; vibrating with shouts and laughter, with sighs and desperation and fear: the last stopover before the long journey.

With a sudden furious movement, Sister Alma flings a towel over the mirrored door of the wardrobe. She removes her coif and sits down. She runs her fingers through her gleaming black hair. She still hasn't shorn it again. I probably look like a clown with these strands sticking up in the air, she thinks.

She should have inquired long ago when the next ship leaves for Swakopmund. She had written that she wants to return to her sick patients. Very few of them were actually sick. Most of them lay on their stomachs, with festering welts on their backs that came from the whips and canes of the German farmers. Dr. Heinrich tried to convince them to stop using the sharp-edged, cracked hippopotamus whips at the very least.

Too much loss of epidermis, he was wont to say. But on the other hand, the use of canes results in liver damage and broken bones. And rope ends? The skin remains unscathed on the surface, but underneath they rupture the muscle tissue.

But how else is one to spread Christianity and civilization?

The wounds were inflicted in the name of Christ, and in the name of Christ they were healed by her. The farmers expected her to nurse the blacks to the point that they were fit to work for them again, and that as soon as possible. She had to fight for every single day a black worker was allowed to remain in her ward at the missionary station.

She often stood outside at night in the semidesert beneath the splendor of the stars, and sometimes she said to herself: This is how your life is passing by.

It's not your life, she then reproached herself. Christ has lent it to you, and you give it back to him.

Did he give it to you so you could help these guys pillage the country and turn free people into slaves? The towel over the mirrored door bothers her all of a sudden. She puts her coif back on and removes the towel.

She cautiously approaches the rickety dresser upon which her roommate has spread out her toiletries: brushes, combs, a hand mirror, a powder tin, perfume flacons, lipstick. What do I really know about people? she asks herself.

She sits down again. She realizes that she is waiting for her roommate to return. When you get right down to it, I was always alone, she thinks.

Her roommate cries out when she enters the room and turns on the light.

My God, you certainly gave me a fright, Mrs. Ebel exclaims. What are you doing sitting there in the dark like that?

Mrs. Ebel is a plump, cheerful, chipper person. She is from Mainz, and although she has a certain sad undertone in her voice, she constantly praises this city to the skies; so much so that Sister Alma finally asks: Why don't you go back there then?

Oh, I can never show my face *there* again, she merrily replies.

Don't you have relatives, friends there?

Oh yes, Mrs. Ebel says. I've got two children there. Egon, he's eight, and Amalie is twelve. I've even got a husband there.

I'm afraid I don't understand.

Of course not, my dear, says Mrs. Ebel. But in order for you to understand, I have to explain a word to you that you don't know. You see, I've run off. Eloped.

As a matter of fact, Sister Alma does not know that word. Once Mrs. Ebel has explained its meaning to her, she asks a question that Mrs. Ebel naturally has anticipated.

With whom? Amalie's piano teacher.

He must be a very impressive man, says Sister Alma, at a loss.

He is twenty, Mrs. Ebel dryly replies.

They don't say anything for a while; then Mrs. Ebel says: But he's an angel. They lapse into silence again.

An angel?

Finally, Mrs. Ebel begins to describe her angel, from head to toe and everything in between, to be exact. Her description is such that Sister Alma is tempted to reach for her prayer book more than once. It turns out that Mrs. Ebel's angel is of a very different nature than the angels that populate Sister Alma's imagination. In a fit of chaste levity, she leans forward and giggles: I'd like to meet him sometime, too.

Mrs. Ebel laughs at the beet-red nun.

Can't be done, can't be done, she exclaims.

And why not?

He's run off on me, says Mrs. Ebel. With all my money. That is, with all the money I gave him: eight thousand marks. What he didn't know — and maybe he would have stuck around a bit longer if he did — is that I've got another twelve thousand hidden in my corset.

Sister Alma takes a deep breath.

Was your husband mean to you? she asks. Maybe he drank.

Oh no, Mr. Ebel is an absolute gem, a sweetheart, declares

82

Mrs. Ebel. And a wonderful building contractor. I really couldn't complain.

And the children?

Yes, the children, says Mrs. Ebel.

They fall silent once again.

But then how do you explain all that? asks Sister Alma. And don't give me the story about your angel again.

But there is no other explanation, don't you see, says Mrs. Ebel seriously.

Sister Alma wakes up during the night. She stares into the darkness, and suddenly she thinks: That would be like me running off on Christ.

Dr. Werth is in incredibly high spirits. He sings in the bathtub; he whistles while putting on a tie; he hums a little tune while spraying himself with cologne.

That must be one hot date you're off to, his mother says suspiciously.

Date? I'm going to Wormser and his Jewish Relief Society, her son replies.

He's never lied before, she thinks. That's odd. Something definitely has happened.

Albert Werth can't explain his good mood to himself either. Even he noticed it. Oh well, you don't need to have an explanation for everything, he thinks.

Mr. Voss, the spice merchant, has sent him a small sandalwood box from the warehouse city; it is full of spice samples. He smells inside it every now and then. It is sitting on top of his desk, ready for the sniffing any time.

He hurriedly traverses the foyer in silence. In the stairwell, however, he whistles to himself once again.

Surely that doctor forgot about his promise long ago, says Ruth. Simon is convinced of the same as well.

He'll come, says Sister Alma.

How do you know that?

I just know, she says.

And where are we going to find another doctor?

He'll show up, believe me, she says, and she can't help but smile.

She is right. There is a knock on the door at just about four on the dot.

Dr. Werth enters the room with a veritable bounce in his step. Instead of going over to his patient, he approaches Sister Alma with an extended hand, almost as if he wants to congratulate her. He notes the hot water, soap, and towels she has set out with appreciation.

Sister Alma explains where she has been and what she has been doing for the past five years.

I'll go ahead and open the window, she says, and to Ruth, Simon, and Daniel: You'll probably want to hold your noses.

Ruth has to turn herself so that her leg is hanging over the edge of the bed a bit. Sister Alma is holding a gauze bandage at the ready. Werth puts the scalpel to Ruth's leg. But then he hesitates. She looks at him, and she realizes that he's doing something like this for the first time; that he's a beginner.

She nods at him in encouragement. Now.

Daniel cries out in disgust. It stinks.

Sister Alma works quickly and skillfully. She discovers a black speck in the wound. Werth gets hold of it with a pair of tweezers. He removes a black splinter of wood from the tissue. Sister Alma bandages the wound. Once they are done washing their hands, they stand facing each other.

Well, I guess I'll be on my way then, says Dr. Werth.

Sister Alma accompanies him out of the room. They stand facing each other again in the hallway.

Have you at least seen a little of Hamburg yet? asks Werth.

She smiles and shakes her head.

May I be permitted to show you a bit of the city?

Why not? And so Dr. Werth and Sister Alma set out on a sightseeing tour in an open hackney — a young man and a nun in full Dominican habit who are very obviously out for a spin, since they aren't in any great hurry to be moving forward. The nun has leaned back in a comfortable position, with her left arm extended on the backrest, and she looks at the hustle and bustle of carriages and passersby with interest and pleasure.

And that is how Tatlin happens to spot her.

They are about midway down Jungfernstieg, and Werth is just pointing out the Alster lake, full of barges and sailboats. Tatlin stops in his tracks. He is jostled, but barely notices that. He is busy observing the two.

When the hackney jogs along toward the market square Gänsemarkt, Tatlin follows it. Werth has the cab pull up in front of a café and pays the coachman. The two disappear into the café. Through the decorative vines that have been etched into the windowpanes, Tatlin catches another glimpse of them as they sit down at a table; then he moves on.

Sister Alma has never been in a café before, never mind in such a den of sensual pleasures as this. Carpeting, marble, mahogany, silver. A café violinist is playing bawdy melodies. Laced-up women with projecting hats and hips; mustaches, side whiskers, goatees, imperial beards. Pomade. Dr. Werth, it may be noted, is clean-shaven.

He hands her the menu.

But what on earth is sherry? Or Cointreau? Or Danziger Goldwasser? Coffee and tea, that's all she knows. She is about to order a coffee when Dr. Werth says: Perhaps a chocolate?

She nods. Although: Is she supposed to eat a bar of chocolate? She did see chocolate once before, those thin slabs.

The waiter returns with a coffee and a cognac for Dr. Werth, and a small pot of hot chocolate for Sister Alma.

He pours it for her; she swallows a little bit: A sweet heaven unfolds. Angels are dancing on her tongue. She takes only tiny sips.

Tatlin strides through the streets as if something at his back is driving him forward. He is in his element in the darkness. The illuminated windows excite him. One cannot see out of a lighted room into the darkness. But one can indeed look into a lighted room from one's vantage point in the dark. The city generates tremendous currents of energy that penetrate his being. He doesn't have any skin; he cannot defend himself against all this wild shouting, laughing, and bellowing that is taking place behind these illuminated windows, behind these doors, in these ballrooms and boudoirs, in these cellars. Wherever he is, that's where he wants to get away from. Wherever he was, that's where he wants to go to. He knows that he will not be able to settle down; he simply cannot stop walking.

There is some kind of commotion in the room. Despite the fact that it is totally silent, there is a commotion going on in the room. It must be about two in the morning. Mrs. Ebel returned to the room an hour ago. After that, Sister Alma fell asleep. But this commotion has caused her to wake up. She really couldn't say exactly what this commotion consists of, because it is completely silent.

Suddenly, she hears breathing: a deep inhaling of air. Then a strained exhaling. Repeatedly. Then a relieved exhaling.

She lies perfectly still on her back. She has closed her eyes. She squeezes her eyelids tightly together. Yet tears well up from under them and run down her cheeks all the same.

9

The dress

Crown, pavilion, girdle. To Mrs. Ebel her corset.
Klaus Groth is freezing.

One must be able to tell the difference between a white diamond and a white zircon; between pink beryl, pink topaz, pink tourmaline, pink sapphire, or spinel, rose quartz, kunzite, garnet, fire opal, chrysoberyl. Tourmaline occurs in practically every color, and a pale blue stone can be zircon, aquamarine, topaz, apatite, synthetic spinel, or euclase. A white stone can be a diamond, a doublet (a flat, genuine diamond glued onto a synthetic base), or also a white sapphire; a synthetic white sapphire, a synthetic rutile (usually a yellowish color), a titanite, a white spinel (rare), white topaz, quartz, or rock crystal. Malachite, idocrase, peridot, citrine, and chrysoprase have started to be employed again lately.

Ruth Kantor doesn't like the way Simon talks about gems. His voice takes on a kind of coldness, and it becomes as hard as the stones he is talking about.

The brilliant-cut diamond has fifty-eight facets. The upper section, the crown, consists of thirty-two facets and the table; the lower section, the pavilion, of twenty-four facets; the dividing line (the circumference of the stone) is the girdle.

She doesn't like the fact that he constantly is sticking his nose into this book he purchased, in which gemstones are described and illustrated.

Simon Kantor was in the city, and only now does he think he really and truly knows what tall buildings look like. He also saw the cold fire again. It was sparkling hundredfold in the jewelers' show windows.

Ruth's leg has improved. She can put weight on it again already. Daniel's favorite reading material is the English dictionary that his father bought for him. It borders on a miracle how quickly he learns. And he wants his parents to learn it as well.

He quizzes them, tests them on vocabulary. He starts to form sentences.

The chairs want to dance a waltz.

The lamp is singing its sad song.

Mama's leg is white.

Ruth also doesn't like the fact that Simon recently has begun to sit in the common room with that Tatlin person.

Klaus Groth went home after seeing to the Russians' lodgings in Meyer's emigrants' house. That which he mechanically still thinks of as home is an apartment in the Gängeviertel, the slum quarter that so shocked the famous bacteriologist Robert Koch when he was summoned to Hamburg following the outbreak of the cholera epidemic. Klaus Groth last had been on leave over a year ago, which was long enough for him to perceive the dirt, abject poverty, and decay almost as if he were seeing it through the eyes of a complete stranger to the neighborhood. He didn't remember it being this bad. While climbing up the narrow, grimy staircase, he thought he would suffocate. He knocked on a door and entered without waiting to be asked inside. The man sitting at the kitchen table looked sixty years old. In fact, he was forty-five. Upon seeing his son, he didn't show any reaction. Klaus Groth unbuttoned his jacket and sat down at the table as well.

Have a good time with the Prussians? his father says.

Klaus Groth knows better than to reply.

Outside, it is broad daylight. In this combined kitchen and living room, however, twilight prevails.

His father is a riveter. Ten hours a day, he pounds white-hot rivets as broad as his thumb. Ten hours of excrutiating loudness; a noisy hell. Ten hours in the cold, damp wind that blows up the Elbe. Every day except Sundays.

His father rises to his feet. He lifts himself as if there were weights resting on his shoulders. He goes to the cupboard and gets a bottle of rye and glasses.

Do you know what the famed Mr. Koch called this here?

I read about it in the paper, says Klaus Groth.

People had trampled up the stairs back then. Someone had

knocked on his father's door, and the house superintendent entered almost simultaneously. Behind him were men in black hats and coats. Before the house super could explain anything, the men pushed their way past him into the apartment. They didn't ask Wilhelm Groth's permission, and nobody bothered to tell him what was going on. They looked around these two rooms as if he wasn't even there, and gradually they fell silent. They were struck dumb.

Gentlemen, one of them finally said, I cannot believe that I am in Europe. These are Asian conditions.

It was the renowned Robert Koch, discoverer of the cholera bacillus, who uttered those words, and he knew what he was talking about, because when he couldn't isolate the cholera germ in Cairo, he went on to Calcutta. As he would later write to his fiancée: In neither the Jewish quarter in Prague nor the ghetto in Italy have I run into worse conditions than those found in the workers' accomodations in the Gängeviertel. In no other city have I encountered such unhealthful living quarters, dens of pestilence, and breeding grounds for disease.

Klaus Groth raises his glass and drinks to his father. He thinks: This man's wife has died on him. He doesn't think that the woman was also his own mother. All he thinks is: This man's wife has died on him.

His sister Gertrud makes a noisy entrance. She is eighteen; a loud, pushy thing.

Nice of you to show yourself again.

She could have known that he didn't get any leave.

He gets up. He can tell that they want him to go. He is wearing his good suit and a tie underneath his jacket. He doesn't fit in here.

He takes deep breaths once outside. He goes to the Bellealliance-St., where his older sister lives. She is pleased to see him; she pats his cheek and has him take a seat. Three small children stare at him. Their mother is pregnant again.

Talk to me while I make the coffee, she says.

You talk, Klaus Groth replies.

She lowers the kettle.

Do you really want to know about it?

Yes, says Klaus Groth. Everything.

She comes over to the table and sits down.

Father came home and she wasn't there anymore. She'd been taken away. But nobody knew where to. After three days, I finally found her. But by then, she was already dead.

Groth waits.

She was lying on the floor, in a row of others.

She swallows. She tries to speak.

I could hardly recognize her, she whispers.

Klaus Groth waits.

They're blue, and twisted, she says. They stare with open eyes and open mouths.

They stink! she screams.

Groth covers her hands with his own. They sit there like that for a while.

Your coffee, she says.

She wants to know what it was like in Berlin, and he talks about it a bit; but in reality, neither one is listening to the other. Finally, he leaves. Neither she nor Gertrud nor his father had asked him what he wanted to do now or where he planned to spend the night.

Mrs. Ebel is in the process of getting dressed. She is walking around the room in a state of dishabille. It appears all the fuss is for a man. Sister Alma is amazed. So that's how it goes. Out with one, in with the other.

That's not how it is, Sister, Mrs. Ebel calls out. It's much more complicated than that. But you haven't any idea what it's all about. And besides, you'd have to know Mr. Benz to appreciate it. He deals in gems. He's from Idar-Oberstein.

Were gem dealers something special? Where was the logic to that? Sister Alma gazed in astonishment. So that's the kind of stuff women wore under their dresses. Red silk, black lace, openworked garters. The fact that Mrs. Ebel is taking such care to prepare herself for her meeting with this Mr. Benz must then mean that Mr. Benz is going to get to see this lingerie as well.

And Mr. Benz wants to go to America, too? Why?

Do you know what a bill of exchange is? says Mrs. Ebel. A

bill sometimes has the nasty tendency to bounce. Picture a great big rubber ball. First it bounced in Idar-Oberstein, then in Coblenz, then in Cologne, then in Münster, then in Bremen. The police don't like all that bouncing. Now help me with my corset. You have to pull here on these two laces until the edges meet. Then you weave them crisscross through the hooks. Pull, hook, pull, hook, until you get to the top.

Why are you holding your breath? Sister Alma asks.

That's what shapes the line, I mean the waistline. It's what does the trick.

Sister Alma pulls and Mrs. Ebel holds on tight to the foot of the bed.

You think I'm fickle, Mrs. Ebel wheezes. But that's not true.

And what about your husband?

I love him. But I never should have married him.

And what about that man who left you?

I love Franz, too, but I never would have married him.

And what about Mr. Benz?

I don't love him, but I will marry him.

I don't think I want to understand any of this, says Sister Alma.

If I'm not thoroughly mistaken, you're about to understand it, and very soon at that, says Mrs. Ebel.

Sister Alma pulls with all her might.

That's good, Mrs. Ebel calls out.

But that must hurt.

Don't matter, exclaims Mrs. Ebel, straightening up. Her corset creaks.

There is a knock.

There's Benz, Mrs. Ebel cries, and I'm not ready yet.

Sister Alma goes to the door to tell Mr. Benz that, but Mrs. Ebel sings out: Let him come on in.

Benz, Mrs. Ebel calls to him while powdering herself in front of the mirror, that is the jolly Sister Alma.

Mr. Benz is a small, plump, amiable man. He pats Mrs. Ebel's remarkable bottom; then he extends this same hand, with which he just patted that half-naked fanny, to Sister Alma.

Benz is the name, he says.

Sister Alma has turned red. The situation was impossible — here she was, together with this man and the seminude Ebel. Then she had an idea. She willed herself to shake Benz's hand heartily. Maybe she could distract this person's attention from the half-naked Ebel and get the latter to put on some clothes at last.

I hear you deal in gems, she says. I've got something here. Perhaps you could give me some advice.

She goes to the wardrobe and returns with a small box. She displays its contents on the table: her aunt's jewelry.

What is this worth?

Mr. Benz whistles through his teeth.

A substantial amount, he says.

How much?

That depends. Give me a piece of paper and a pencil, Mr. Benz replies, and he starts to assess the jewelry piece by piece. Once he is done adding up the numbers, he says: Well, a jeweler would net about fifty-two thousand eight hundred for that. If you sold that to him on the other hand, you'd get maybe five thousand.

Thank you, says Sister Alma. She puts the jewelry back in the box. Mrs. Ebel is finally ready, and the two say goodbye.

Although Mrs. Werth had yet to make breakfast for her son, she always kept him company during it. How else was she to make sure he ate properly?

You were seen, she says.

Albert Werth taps the crown of his boiled egg with a spoon.

With a mulatto woman.

How very interesting, replies Albert Werth. The egg is exactly how he likes it.

Right off the boat from Caracas.

That had quite a ring to it: a mulatto from Caracas.

And you strolled down Jungfernstieg with her on your arm.

First of all, says Albert Werth, I did not walk down Jungfernstieg with her, but rather I drove down it in an open hackney. Secondly, she was not a mulatto, but rather a German Dominican nun. And thirdly, she is not from Caracas, but rather she is returning to her missionary station in Africa.

But you're hiding *something*, she exclaims while leaving the room. And don't try to tell me otherwise.

Someone from HAPAG had approached him and asked whether he could fill in for a ship's doctor who had taken ill. Just for one journey: New York and back. He'd asked for time to think about it. His mother would have an absolute fit if he accepted. Ship's doctor — that came right after taxi dancer in her book.

Tatlin sees Sister Alma standing in front of a fashion store. He sidles up next to her. She looks up. He smiles, but she does not return his smile.

If you don't want to go back to Africa, where do you want to go? he asks.

What makes you think I don't want to go back to Africa?

He smiles and shrugs his shoulders.

And you? she says. You don't know where you want to go either.

A small, severe-looking wrinkle has appeared between her eyebrows.

Oh yes I do, he replies. To America.

I wish you a pleasant afternoon then, she says, and continues on her way.

Klaus Groth is sitting on the bank of the Elbe in Altona; he looks across the river to the shipyards. He is cold. Something is missing. No matter where he happened to have been in the past, there was always that tiny distant point that radiated warmth. Now all that is there is a cold, empty space.

It starts to sink in that his mother is dead. His older sister had described it for him, but only now does Klaus Groth realize that she is dead. He leaps to his feet and paces back and forth. He suddenly gasps for air. He runs down the steep bank to the Elbe. He stares at the river. Little by little, he manages to push down this rising growth in his chest that threatens to choke him; to squeeze it until it becomes smaller; to force it down into his stomach, where it lodges in the form of a little bitter knot.

Hammer blows that sound as if they were struck by giants ring out from the shipyard across the river. Metal on metal squeals. Chains rattle.

Standing among the afternoon-shift workers on a motor launch, he crosses the river to Blohm & Voss. He wants to go to his father. He leaps over tracks, weaves through cranes, dodges locomotives. The noise is deafening.

He approaches the frigate that is under construction and is lying on its keel: a towering, rust-brown steel hulk. Shouting, he asks one worker after the other the way to his father; he climbs ladders; and finally, he stands before him. His father lowers his riveting hammer.

What do you want? he says.

Only now does he realize that he doesn't know why he went there, and he is ashamed.

I want to say goodbye, he says. I'm going to America.

His father looks at him.

I'd do that, too, if I was as young as you are.

And then his father extends his hand to him. Never, ever had his father touched him, except to hit him.

Klaus Groth grasps his father's hand. For the first time ever, he feels his father's hand in his own; it is hard and heavy. Their handshake lasts a moment too long, but for Klaus Groth, it is a very precious moment indeed. He turns around and climbs down the ladder.

Sitting in the afternoon stillness of a pub, a beer in front of him, the turmoil within him begins to quiet down. Strange, how he came to say that he was going to America. He'd never given it a moment's thought until he'd said that. Had he said it out of shame, because he had run to his father and didn't know why? Out of spite? There was no reason he couldn't go to America; he had the money for it.

He is cold. He needs a place to sleep. And so he heads for Meyer's emigrants' house. When Groth appears in the doorway of the dormitory, Tatlin spots him right away and waves. Here's a free bed.

Thyme and sage and pepper and cardamom: Albert Werth has not forgotten that he has to look in on Ruth Kantor to see how she is progressing. And then he has an idea. When he knocks on the door of room number sixteen at four on the dot and enters, he is carrying something that a leading Hamburg delicatessen refers to as a gift basket, and which the less refined would simply call a basket full of eats. It contains ham and sausages and cans of pâté de foie gras and caviar; champagne and cognac and grapes and cheese. Dr. Werth makes a buoyant entrance, but then he sees at once that Sister Alma is not there. Disappointed, he deposits the basket on the table.

How's the leg doing? he says to Ruth. Still having problems with the knee?

And then he sees the tall, thin woman in a red dress with a black floral design; she is also wearing a soft black hat on her head.

But don't you recognize me anymore? she asks. It's me.

Albert Werth stares. He is growing hot.

Sister Alma.

My name is Alma Laufer, the woman says with a smile.

The knee's fine, says Ruth Kantor. And the wound is already starting to close.

They have themselves a regular feast. They get Mrs. Ebel and Benz to join them, and finally Tatlin and Groth, too.

It sure is hot in here, Tatlin says upon entering the room.

It is not hot in here, Alma retorts without looking at him. You've got a fever.

How do you know that? he says.

I can see that you do, she replies.

Without looking at me? he thinks.

When they run out of champagne, Groth is sent to get beer.

How about a cup of hot chocolate? says Albert Werth.

Alma Laufer shakes her head with a smile. Not this time.

95

10

Confessions

Daniel is allowed to sleep at Mama's side.
Klaus Groth must go far, far away.
Sister Alma moves.

They killed my mother. They killed almost ten thousand people. Something's happened to me. I'm still not sure what. They killed something inside me, too.

They've got their own wells. Their servants boil the water for them so it's germ-free. But we have to drink the infected water. They could have filtered it through sand, but that was too expensive for them. Everything that could benefit us is too expensive. We eat too much, we take up too much room, we breathe too much. We cost too much. And we never work enough.

Out on Brook island, they threw twenty-four thousand people out of their homes. They needed room for the warehouse city. They needed room for the wares. They didn't give a damn where those twenty-four thousand people were supposed to go.

I was a second lieutenant's orderly in Berlin. I heard the second lieutenants talking. If what they're expecting to happen happens, then there's going to be a war, and then millions will die. They can't even be bothered to spare a single thought about that.

Sand filters don't cost a lot. They installed them in Bremen, and there wasn't even a single case of cholera there. Here, it took them ten days just to admit that there's an epidemic in the city. It might be bad for business. Yeah, and where in the city was the epidemic? It was where us poor working stiffs live, not in their villas and mansions. Cholera is a prole disease.

When you gotta lug around sacks for twelve hours a day, you don't waste much time thinking about the future. You're too damn tired for that. Army life was like paradise at first. Clean clothes, clean beds, clean dorms. No lice or bedbugs or rats. And plenty to eat. The little bit of marching and drills was no sweat. And shooting was fun. They even sent me to learn how to be a sharpshooter. I finally had time to think straight in the army.

Something's wrong with me. I realize now how often I used to think of her, how I used to think, You have to tell her that; You gotta show her that; What will she think of that? Like a little kid that runs up and wants to give her something, that wants something, wants to show something off.

Maybe it'd be different if she'd died normal, from some other illness. But like this, it was murder. They took her away from me. I'm not even angry or sad. That's all behind me. I'm just freezing cold. I got this feeling I'm gonna do something sometime. I don't know what yet, but any day now, I'm gonna do something.

I think you'd better go away from here, Tatlin says. You need to go far away, and real soon.

Ruth has bought something for Daniel.

He starts to hop up and down. For me?

He fingers the package. It feels soft.

It's probably something to wear, he says disappointedly.

Unwrap it, says Ruth.

He opens the paper. Something flowery, in red and blue and black. Made of cloth. He picks it up gingerly. It unfurls: a dress. A girl's dress.

He stares at it in disgust.

Take off your jacket and trousers, says Ruth.

What's this all about? says Simon Kantor.

Ruth determinedly removes her son's jacket and trousers. When she attempts to pull the dress over his head, he screams and ducks under the table.

Would you please tell us what is going on here, demands Simon Kantor, and this time, he means business.

Tomorrow we have to go into the emigrants' huts. And he is not going into the men's dorm with you. He's staying with me.

Daniel is squatting under the table. He pricks up his ears. Lately he has been having trouble falling asleep, and that was strange. Although he obediently went to bed and closed his eyes like he was supposed to, whenever his mother or father would say, Do you think he's asleep now?, he was overcome by insuppressible fits of coughing. His parents are fighting above him. They're fighting because of him. He listens with a small, self-satisfied smile on his face.

But he's a boy, he has to sleep in the men's dorm, his father says.

With all those hairy, tobacco-chewing, spitting criminals? With those roughnecks and stinking boors? his mother exclaims. He'll sleep next to me.

Daniel hadn't thought that far ahead, crouched there under the table. This was most interesting. He cautiously pokes his head out from under the table.

He's staying with me and that's that, his mother cries. Come here.

She drags him out of his hiding place and pulls the dress over his head as if she's capturing him. She plucks at the material some, then takes a step back.

Daniela, she calls out. Isn't she sweet?

Daniel looks at his father. With a triumphant little smile on his face, he pulls the dress a bit to the left and curtsies.

Where I come from, the sun is still the only clock for most people, although here and there, church bells do divide up the time a bit more precisely. But there were some clocks there, too. Kitchen timers, alarm clocks, pocket watches — but the pocket watches were worn more or less for decoration. I knew that the further west I went, the more the clock density would increase. More and more people were guided by one and the same measurement of time. And then I saw my first station clock. With that, the railroad doesn't just commit itself to being punctual, it also obliges the passengers to be punctual as well. And as I was sitting there over my watches, I had a vision. The cycle of trains would become ever more finely tuned to the comings and goings of the ships, and this would be coordinated with the flow of goods from the factories and people's time of work and rest. Everything is well thought-out, with one thing leading to the other; it's all finely tuned and adjusted — one big, harmonious cycle, where there would be no room for anything that's useless and foolish. The world as a clockwork.

Until they tried to kill us.

We ran. Ever since then, I know what it's like to fear death. But since then, I also know I will do anything necessary to make sure something like that never happens to me again. And when I say anything, I do mean anything.

Bravo, says Tatlin. That's the right attitude to go to New York with.

My God, now you've gone and frightened me again, Sister, says Mrs. Ebel upon entering the room. What are you doing sitting there like that? Two suitcases and your nun get-up again.

I didn't want to leave without saying goodbye, says Sister Alma. I'm switching hotels. I don't want anyone to be able to find me.

What you're trying to hide from already found you a long time ago, says Karoline Ebel, removing her hat and coat.

It hits you out of the blue, says Mrs. Ebel. It goes against all reason, and sometimes I think it doesn't matter if it's this man or that one. Do you think I was able to choose my Franz?

What's worse than their cruelty is that they have a clear conscience while they're beating them, says Sister Alma. They don't feel guilty; it's the exact opposite — they're actually proud that they're teaching the blacks what work is.

Do you think I didn't know what it meant to start something with Franz? Do you think I didn't love my children? What I did to them is a crime.

Brutality, hypocrisy — what business of mine would it be if all that didn't occur in the name of God, if the church that I'm part of didn't approve of it?

I tried to fight it, says Karoline Ebel. You can't leave your children and your husband, you can't run away. You have to fight. Until I saw that if I won that fight, it would be at the price that I'm dead. Dead in a living body.

I need to be alone.

You will never be alone again. He is with you. He won't be gotten rid of anymore.

It's always described as being something wonderful, something happy and light.

By idiots. And it only happens to the few. Only a few are capable of it. Only a few have the necessary strength.

It's something horrible, and dark.

It's life.

I tried to pray, until I realized how childish, even blasphemous, it is to reduce God to a benevolent father whom we beg for a present.

That dark and horrible something *is* the present.

It kills.

Not you. I know that I'll never be able to forgive myself for what I've done to my children. And at some point in time, that will kill me. But you are alone and free. You've hit the jackpot.

Mrs. Laufer? says the man, and runs his index finger down the list of names in his register. We don't have any Mrs. Laufer.

The nun. Perhaps you remember, says Albert Werth.

Oh yes, of course. She checked out.

Albert Werth looks at the man as if he didn't understand him. Then he turns around and leaves. He is dazed; it's as if someone had hit him.

Fine, he thinks. Then I'll sign on as ship's doctor. That's just the ticket for me now.

11

Pursuing the pursuer

A postcard gets its revenge. Tatlin throws his knives again. A nun on Jungfernstieg. Dr. Werth fills out a death certificate.

While looking into a shop window displaying men's clothing, Tatlin makes a discovery that causes his scalp to contract and his blood to run cold: Standing next to him and peering into the same window is the forester; the man who had invited him to the hunt, a German named Nemetz.

Tatlin turns his back on the forester and crosses the street. After walking a bit, he stops. Did Nemetz notice him? Tatlin knows why he is in Hamburg. Because of him. Rybakov had sent him. If he can't get back his recruits, then he wants to have the man who stole them from him, if only to have him shot dead.

They'd thought he was finished; that he'd either bled to death in the willow shrub or drowned in the swamp. But in Eydtkuhnen, he was itching for trouble. He couldn't help it — he sent Rybakov a card that said: Before I board the ship for America in Hamburg, I would like to express my most humble thanks for your hospitality following the great battue. An open postcard. One that the postmaster, the mailman, and the servants naturally read. Tatlin grins.

It appears that Nemetz has seen enough at last, and he moves on. Tatlin follows him on the other side of the street. He is pursuing the pursuer. It's the only way to be safe from Nemetz. But it also gives him a thrill.

Why did he write that card? Why did he help those soldiers desert? He earned enough money as a recruiter. Why did he throw his knives at Rybakov's celebration; why didn't he make the forester's wife leave his room? Why don't you join the paper's editorial staff? Sonja's father had asked. In six months' time, you'll be department head. Why don't you come and join us, Tatlin? Father Basilius, his Greek teacher at the Jesuit boarding school in Kraków (and a very elegant man), had asked. We need people like you. What's that little bit of chastity compared to the power, to participating in a great work? People had opened doors for him. But he didn't go through a single one.

Nemetz appears to have a goal. He pulls out his watch, puts it away again, and continues on his way at a faster pace. Finally, he disappears inside a pompous and self-important building located on a side street. There is a shiny brass plate on its door: Russian Consulate General. On the other side of the street, Tatlin takes up his post diagonally opposite the edifice.

He has had a dream. He threw his knives again. But not at the princess; rather, he threw them at that nun.

He was sure that he hadn't taken note of Hamburg while on his way to America the first time. Now, he constantly experiences déjà vu. These church steeples; this water in the middle of the city; the Elbe full of steamers and tugboats and motor launches all seem familiar to him. He was supposed to go on ahead, she would come later; that's what they had said. When he saw her in Kraków on the arm of his friend, he was filled with a burning and lurid illumination: That had been a ruse of hers to get rid of him. Now, however, another thought, this one cold and tenacious, had entrenched itself in his mind: Was it in fact the opposite; had he been the one who was fleeing from her? He did not return her kisses; he had tolerated them. And yet, he longed for them. He is convinced that he was never in love, hot and cold as the mythical salamander.

Nemetz leaves the building. There is a man with him. Both walk up the street resolutely.

It seemed Tatlin couldn't stop thinking about his father lately. He didn't have many memories of situations in which his parents were together, but there was one memory that recurred over and over again. In it, his father was overcome by a whim, a capricious mood, and he began to dance around his wife; he whistled popular songs; he sang operetta tunes in which some prince swore his love to his sweetheart. His mother's eyes became hard with rejection. She drew herself up and made herself even more unapproachable than she already was. Oh no you don't, she was saying, it's not that simple. Especially when you can't even pay your bills.

At such moments, he thought his mother a perfect scream. Her righteousness, her respectability, her standoffishness. And he suspected that his father felt the same way; that he actually sang his operetta arias to provoke that reaction in her, so that both of them, father and son, could be amused at her expense. But perhaps an eleven-year-old simply cannot comprehend that an adult is being serious when he sings: You are my whole life. Wherever you are not, I cannot be.

Why did he send Rybakov that card? Why did he think that his mother was so funny? Why was he unable to resist any opportunity to make fun of her respectability, of her bills and rules, of that which they called reality?

Nemetz and his escort are headed for a building with the words Police Station above the door. They go inside. Now he's looking to the Germans for back-up, Tatlin thinks.

But had he not acted just as cool to Sonja as his mother had to his father? If he had been unable to understand as an eleven-year-old what it meant for someone to sing You are my whole life, was he able to understand it now? It had been sheer torture for him when, in New York, he had sat in front of a blank sheet of paper and was supposed to answer her letters. In flowing, well-formed sentences, she declared her love for him. He, however, chewed on his fountain pen. Could one even speak of love? Wasn't that already a betrayal of it? Hypocrite, he said to himself. You don't even know what that is. You're like a blind man talking about color.

Whose idea had it really been to go to America? His or hers? And what did they want over there? Were things so much better there? There, they could be together, they could marry; here, she had been promised to a cloth millowner. But wouldn't Germany or France have done? Why America? He lets the word America roll on his tongue, and then he realizes that he was the one who had suggested it. Which meant that he had run from her.

Nemetz exits the door of the police station. With him are the man from the consulate and a third man, apparently a German plainclothesman. They set off in the direction of the port. Tatlin follows them. He is safest when he is behind his pursuers. The three men enter a boardinghouse. Now they're inspecting the register, thinks Tatlin. They can search for my name forever. Naturally, he was traveling with phony identification papers.

If he had fled to America, from what had he been fleeing? From her? From her demand for love? Because he couldn't meet it? Even if one could say that was the case, and one could not, why did he come back? What had catapulted him back and forth like that?

The three men leave the rooming house, cross the street, and vanish inside a hotel on the other side of the road. Tatlin watches this maneuver take place another two times; then he enters a hotel that they have already checked and asks for a room. He has a bite to eat in the barroom and then goes upstairs. He is tired, as if he has been working; and he is satisfied, as if he's done a good job.

In his dream, the nun had stood in front of the same high oaken door as the princess had, but they were in a different location: in a hall that was reminiscent of a nave. And they had been alone. There was an echo whenever a knife lodged in the wood of the door. The palms of her hands were exposed and turned toward him. She smiled, and he threw the knives with her consent. She trusted him completely. A moment of peace.

Is a woman of the cloth allowed to look at the goods on display in a fashion store? What is she doing on Jungfernstieg in Hamburg anyway? Is she there on business? If so, she would have to be moving with a purpose to her stride. Or is a nun allowed to go for a stroll?

And what happens when she tires and wants to take a rest? Is she allowed to enter a café and sit at one of the free tables? In Munich or Bamberg, people surely would have an opinion on that matter; not so in Hamburg. Nuns are something exotic there. They've only heard one thing about them.

The waiter recognizes Sister Alma at once. He leads her to the very table she had shared with Dr. Werth.

The same thing? he asks with a smile.

Sister Alma blushes. She nods her head.

Only now does she see what kind of place' Dr. Werth had taken her to back then. Had she been dressed in worldly clothes, in those of her aunt for instance, they never would have let her in here. What the ladies have on are not so much dresses as they are proof of solvency; precious installations that must have required at least three lady's maids to get in to, and at least that many to get out of. Plush and marble everywhere, and above all: mirrors. They turn the rooms into great halls.

She has difficulty finding a spot where she can't see herself reflected. A nun in a mirror — that is a contradiction in terms; it's a sin. Ever since she was in her aunt's house, she's been fighting with mirrors. She had ignored them; she had covered them; she had tried to see only her face whenever she happened to be forced to look in one. Or caught herself looking in one. Yet she had lost the battle. The first time was in her aunt's house, when she had held up the dress that she wanted to bring back for Mathilde, and then in the hotel room she had shared with that woman.

The waiter brings the chocolate. He pours it for her. She nods. She does not look at him, but she blushes again nevertheless.

There had been no avoiding it in that cramped little room, and Mrs. Ebel was standing in front of the mirror all the time.

How the chocolate smells! She puts off taking the first sip. She prepares herself for it.

Mrs. Ebel had a body. That was obvious. But did she have a body, too? Her habit not only concealed it; it downright denied it. She had only the vaguest of notions of her body. Whenever she washed herself with soap and cloth, she kept on her loose slip, as she had been ordered to do. She had never seen herself naked. On the afternoon when Dr. Werth had come to look in on Ruth Kantor's leg for the second time, she had taken advantage of Mrs. Ebel's absence to wash herself. But when she went to put on her heavy habit again, she suddenly had reached for the dress that she wanted to give Mathilde. She hastily slipped it on, put on that black hat, and ran, even fled, to the Kantors' room.

Did the dress look good on her? Didn't she look grotesque, ridiculous in it? She hadn't looked in the mirror. But she didn't need a mirror. The eyes of Ruth Kantor and Simon and Dr. Werth had been mirror enough. It looked good on her. It looked very good on her.

She had returned to her room. She stood in front of the mirror. And then she had removed the dress, slip and all. For the first time ever, she had seen her body.

Sister Alma carefully raises the cup to her lips. She reverentially takes the first sip.

Tatlin steps out of the hotel and into the street; it's a moment that he loves. A light, patchy cover of clouds over the narrow shaft of the street; the air cool and a little smoky. A horse-drawn carriage with sacks of coal; one of the horses tosses its head. A woman crosses the street with a basket on her arm. Her apron is as long as her skirt. Two dogs chase each other in a circle. The whole day lies before him, long and wide and incalculable.

One thing, however, is sure: Three men are looking for him. Six eyes, but in reality just two, since Nemetz is the only one who knows what he looks like.

They were not respected people, the Tatlins. A child picks up on something like that quickly. How the stableboys looked at each other when his father gave them instructions and then continued on his way. They didn't say anything; they simply looked at each other, and sometimes they would smirk at each other. Or how people stopped talking, or changed the subject, when he came within earshot. Or the exaggerated merriment that broke out when he joined other estate owners. He didn't fit in with them. He was too clever, too imaginative, and not greedy enough. Sometimes he sparkled with wit. But he could seem a bit ridiculous at times, too. And sometimes desperate as well.

His wife was feared and disdained. Her husband runs around on her, remarked the others (whose own husbands ran around on them, too) disparagingly; and thus, little Tatlin found it more and more difficult to go into the village. The fury with which packs of children persecuted him told him how they talked about his parents. The village became something to avoid.

The Jesuit boarding school in Kraków cured him of this timidity. He will never forget the moment when he first entered the dormitory and all eyes were upon him. They beat him; they raped him; they humiliated him. After six months, he had developed an aggressiveness that could no longer be broken, no matter how much they hit him. He blew up at the slightest provocation. He hit them back until he drew blood. He went after students who were a head taller than he. It seemed that he knew no pain, and no fear. They began to be afraid of him. Eventually, they left him alone, and he was free to develop a cheerful, equable cynicism.

All of a sudden, Tatlin found himself standing in front of the forester. They were so startled that neither one of them could move. They stared at each other. And then Tatlin was overcome by an incredible and totally irrepressible fit of laughing. He ran and laughed at the same time. He laughed until his sides ached. He ran behind a streetcar that had just started off, caught up to it, and hauled himself up on to the platform. At the next stop, he switched to another line, and then to another at the stop following that, and all the while, this laughter kept tickling him. He rode to the last station on the route, a village far beyond the outskirts of Hamburg, although the streets had been paved already and excavations had been dug. At the edge of a pasture, he plunked himself down in the grass.

Sister Alma is sitting in St. Katharinen. A Catholic nun in a Protestant church. She is alone. The noise of the city is far away. Muffled like that, it only made the silence deeper. She wants to pray. Does she want to ask for something? That suddenly seems childish to her, diminishing God. Does she want to worship? Then she would need to form a picture of HIM. But, beyond every notion, beyond every concept, where *could* He be found — so hidden and obscure?

When she had first arrived in Karibib, a woman had looked after her; she was Mrs. Baumgart, the wife of a farmer. She had Sister Alma over to their house; gave her advice; told her about the country and the blacks. Together with her husband and their three children, she lived in an impressive house in the middle of a large farm not far from Karibib. She was a blonde, resolute woman, who was nevertheless sometimes capable of a surprising sensitivity and warmth. Compared to her liveliness, her husband seemed quiet and serious. Poetry and music were his great love. He had sent for a piano and notes, and on certain evenings or afternoons, he gave regular concerts. But they also sang, together with their children, various songs; often canons, also choruses in four-part harmony, usually hymns. And in between, there were always games of forfeits, excursions, and tea parties. She was practically one of the family, and for the first time in her life, she had an inkling of what it would be like to have a home.

Until the day that black worker was delivered to her station. His back was one huge wound. And that had been done by Mr. Baumgart and his whip. The same Mr. Baumgart who loved music so much; who could recite poetry in such a way that you thought you would lift right off the ground and float away?

Here she sits, in this Hamburg church. She is in an awful predicament. She cannot go back to Karibib, nor can she return to her mother house. She can't cry. She has folded her hands as if she is praying, but she presses her palms together as if she has to convince herself that she still exists.

Cameria, Acimera, Imeraca. Ameraci, Meracia, Iamerac. — If it was not the case that she had sent Tatlin away, was it then true that he had fled from her? Hadn't he wanted to build her a house on a river?

Igor Tatlin had had a dream; he dreamed it in serial form. He had journeyed far. The distances between the settlements had become greater and greater. And then, next to a river, he had seen the spot. This is where he wanted to build a house, and he knew that this was a place for evermore. Terrific blizzards would come, and scorching summers; but the fish would always swim upriver, the stag would always descend the slope with its head bobbing beneath its heavy antlers, and in the autumn, the salmon would come. They would watch the years go by with serenity, and only measure them by the growth of their children.

In the autumn, they would drive the two-year-old cattle to the small city that was located a couple miles downriver. They know everyone who lives there. In the only store in town, they would buy supplies for the winter, and ammunition, too; that was for the Winchester that hung ready for action on their wall at home — good for bears, bandits, and government officials who wanted to collect taxes and were always blathering on and on about laws. And they would go to the only saloon in the city to have a whiskey as golden brown as the honey that he gets from his bees and that flows so deliciously slowly from the strainer into the jar.

And sometimes during autumn, way up in the vale, when the woods are glowing in shades of red and yellow, he will suddenly find an Indian standing before him. That always happens unexpectedly, because they move as silently as spirits; and they are spirits — the old spirits of this country. They both will bow to each other, because they live in peace.

And then, at some point in time, he will hold her hand during her last hour and help her across. Afterwards, he would go out into the storm and lie down in the snow. It would be the happiest hour of his life. America, the land in which love succeeds.

Tatlin never got to see his river and his valley. He had seen the Bowery and the Lower East Side instead. And he wants to go back there despite that fact? He wants to go back there for that very reason.

The scream is such that the desk clerk drops his fountain pen right away and storms up the stairs. A woman is lying on the floor in front of a door that is partially open. He glances inside the room, flinches, and closes the door. The woman on the ground appears to be unconscious. People come running from all directions. They pour water into her mouth. She gradually regains consciousness, but still cannot speak.

By the time Dr. Werth arrives, someone has already cut the body from the window cross in the room and placed it on the bed. Her neck mercifully has been covered with a scarf. He pronounces her dead, but in order to fill out the death certificate, he needs the woman's personal data. He rummages around in her handbag and finds her passport at last: Ebel, Karoline.

12

The accordion

Daniel says farewell to Natasha.
Simon Kantor learns how to play skat.
What the dog tax is good for.

Residents of Hamburg like to take their out-of-town guests to one of the scenic cafés on the banks of the Elbe in the neighborhoods of Övelgönne or Teufelsbrück, where they can watch the numerous ships plying the river. While one sits there enjoying coffee and cake, a huge ocean liner may float by outside. What makes this sight unique is that experience tells us structures of this enormous size are heavy and immovable (city blocks, town halls, churches); here, however, they turn out to be mobile. This generally causes a great deal of confusion in the observers, but they seem to find it amusing, because they usually express their bewilderment in the form of surprised and enthusiastic shouts. Later, when they write their postcards, they refer to the ships gliding past as "majestic".

Two sturdy tugboats are towing the *Saxonia* up the Elbe. She is returning from a voyage to New York. On her passage to America, she was carrying people on board, most of them emigrants; on her return voyage, she is loaded with goods. She will moor in the Brooktorhafen section of the port.

Simon Kantor is sitting in front of a blank sheet of paper. Next to the piece of paper is an envelope. He is chewing on his pencil. To whom does he want to write a letter?

When they had packed in preparation for moving to the emigrants' huts, Ruth had slipped the girl's dress over Daniel's head at the very end. They hadn't had any time to wonder why he didn't protest, even when Ruth had tied together his hair over his ears in two braidlike pigtails.

Simon Kantor regarded his son with amusement.

Our Daniela, he exclaimed.

Daniel just looked at him.

And as if that was not ridicule enough, he added: Now you can't pee standing up anymore either. He even laughed at his own joke.

Daniel blushed and lowered his gaze.

When they set out, he stuck very close to his mother, and once she finally had a free hand in all the commotion and yelling of the huts, he took it and would not let go of it anymore. It was afternoon by the time they were done with the examinations and formalities at last, and were able to look for a bed in the women's dorm and settle in a bit. Until then, they had thought that Daniel's quiet docility was his way of trying to help them, and they had been relieved. But when he continued his silence even after supper, Ruth looked at him pensively.

Don't you feel well? Say something.

He pressed his lips together and shook his head. A little while later, he pulled her head down to his and whispered something in her ear. She got up and went to the lavatories with him. They had to wait. When one of the wooden stalls finally opened up, she sent him inside. On the way back to the hut where the meals were served, he grabbed her hand again immediately.

Something was wrong with him. His hand lay small and hot within her own, and the way he sat there all silent and still, he wasn't himself. Could a girl's dress possess such powers of transformation? Or was he afraid of the noise and confusion in the huts? Up till now, he had never been all that timid. But she didn't press him any further. Whatever was causing him to be so quiet would reveal itself eventually.

It revealed itself when they went to go to bed. It had been a long time since Ruth Kantor had shared a bed with her son. He was much too old for that; and as if to say he thought so, too, he lay at the very edge of the mattress, stiffly and on his back, completely isolated and alone. Ruth leaned over to him.

Daniel, she whispered. What's wrong?

When he didn't respond, she started to turn him toward her, and only then did she notice the tension in his body. She edged up closer to him.

Daniel, she whispered.

He remained silent, yet she could feel that something inside him was getting ready; something was welling up within him.

Daniel.

And then, it broke through. Not in the form of crying, not in the form of sobbing; rather, it broke through in the form of a dry, disconsolate whimpering.

She held him tight.

Natasha.

The word came out as a whimper.

She pressed him closer.

Natasha. He began to sob.

Finally, he cried. And while he cried, the tension in his body lessened. She clasped his head to her breast. Natasha hadn't wanted to sit next to him in the classroom anymore. She held him close; at last his tears dried up, and his body went limp and soft. His breathing became regular, and then he fell asleep.

Why had he been crying? That girl had betrayed him. Right now, he still thinks of her as his friend. Many years from now (provided life has not been too hard on him and made him callous and unfeeling), he will realize, perhaps on some bleak and gloomy Sunday afternoon, that she was in fact his first, his true, his only love — a rapture never felt since. And he will recognize it by the pain that is suddenly fresh and inconsolable, as it had been in the arms of his mother, even though he is now an old man.

He wasn't crying because of Natasha's betrayal; he had forgiven that long ago. He was crying because he had lost her for all time; because, once they had crossed the ocean, there was no turning back. He cried out of longing.

Simon Kantor brooded over his blank piece of paper. Hadn't he been betrayed as well? Everyone in the small town had known him. But not a one had come to his aid. If he now wanted to write to those people so far beyond the horizon, did that mean he had forgiven them? Anyone who can even ask such a question has no idea what longing means.

Ruth discovered him sitting there in front of the blank sheet of paper.

113

Who do you want to write to?

I don't know.

She took the piece of paper and tore it to shreds.

You aren't going to write to anyone.

She didn't know to whom he had wanted to write. But she knew why he wanted to write. She herself thought, felt, and dreamed about back there. That was because images were constantly rising to the surface, and with them: colors, odors, sounds and noises. The creaking of the harvest wagon; the voices of mothers calling the family in to dinner; the crowing of the roosters. The rain on the windowpanes. The crackling of snow. The steady passing of time. The graves.

She had no illusions. That is where the indifferent and the evil were; that is where friends were. But that is also where they had had the right to live, there in that small, poor town — at least, that is what they had thought. The right to belong, to be at home there, and, someday, to die there. Now, so far removed from that place, she came to realize that images first develop their power to seduce — that eerie life of their own, their otherworldly shining — through loss.

Daniel awoke in his mother's arms, and it was as if he had survived some horrible illness. He lay there weak and lightheaded and happy. His mother was still asleep; he did not move so he wouldn't wake her.

At breakfast, his appetite amazed everybody. That did not prevent him, however, from asking for another piece of bread. Afterwards, he retired to bed again.

Leaning against the wall, with his legs pulled up to his chest, he sat there at the head of the bed, full, satisfied, and still a little weak. He looked around him, and slowly, as if he had lost the ability to do so, like someone who had been in a dead faint, he began to see again: the children running around and chasing each other; the voices and the commotion in the room. And this weakness that was still inside him began to vanish; he got his strength back; and suddenly, he pulled the dress over his head and flung it away from him. He was his old self again: Daniel Kantor. He jumped up and ran over to a group of boys his own age.

You can't just sit around here all glum like that, Ruth exclaimed. Why don't you play something? Chess, for example. So the time goes by faster and you have some kind of diversion.

Good idea, said Klaus Groth; he rooted around in his seabag and finally threw a pack of playing cards on the table.

Skat! called out Robert Benz, his voice tingling with excitement.

But I don't know how to play that, said Simon Kantor.

That doesn't matter, replied Robert Benz, it's easy to learn. We'll show you how.

Ruth left the three men alone.

Daniel wandered to and fro. Alone, or together with other boys. He had forgotten about last night's events. He had forgotten Natasha as well. However, there were not many opportunities to play or discover anything new in the overcrowded huts; on top of that, the German officials were Draconically strict. This meant they soon grew bored. They began to quarrel; the older children whiled away the time by picking on the younger kids; and so Daniel decided to withdraw from their company. But where was he supposed to go instead? His father was playing that baffling card game skat. That left only his mother.

Skat is a ritual, and rituals are good for relieving both boredom and fear. The shuffling, the dealing, the discarding. Picking up your hand, arranging your hand, evaluating your hand. Running through all the possibilities, speculating on the Bockround. And no matter what your hand is like, under no circumstances are you allowed to show any reaction (unless it consists of a smart-alecky or vindictive smile). It's a different story when you've got a Grand with 4, game 5, schwarz 6. But then, as with Null Ouvert, you throw your whole hand down on the table after the first trick. Resistance is pointless.

The three men are sitting inside an invisible house. Ukrainian farmers in high fur hats, knee-length jackets, and knee boots; Poles in low shoes and round hats; Russians in knickerbockers and jackboots; women carrying children in their arms, their head scarves slung around their chests; the yelling and the bickering; the irrepressible restlessness of the children — none of that makes any impression on the card players; it is far away. Who dealt? one of them asks after studying his hand, as if he's just awakened. Okay, he says. I'll play Hearts.

Everything that penetrates from beyond the walls of the huts — the noise of the shipyards, voices and shouts — is far off as well. But above all, the muffled, booming calling of the ships. It is calling for them. For the time being, however, what matters is playing out this Clubs game.

Mr. Nussbaum hurries through the emigrants' huts tirelessly. He is well dressed, if a bit fussily (pepper-and-salt, waistcoat, bow tie); on the street or in a café, he would cut a fine figure, but here, among all these Russian, Polish, Ukrainian, and Romanian farmers, craftsmen, and loafers, he is out of place to put it mildly. He moves nimbly and busily. He has urgent business to take care of. But what? People ask themselves that when he's bustled by them for the third time at the latest. He is a steerage passenger like all the rest of them, and like all the rest, he has nothing to do but wait. So to whom is he delivering such apparently urgent messages?

In Versbolovo, before the Prussian border, is where our troubles began, the woman relates. A German doctor and several policemen boarded the train. We were searched, and we had to tell them where we were going and how much money we had. The result of the inquisition: We were only allowed to cross the border if we exchanged our third-class steamer tickets for second-class tickets, which cost two hundred rubles more than we had. They took away our passports and refused to let us go any further.

Daniel is standing next to his mother, who is seated, and is leaning against her shoulder. Among the circle of women is one woman who is nursing her child; he follows this with a kind of dreamy, faraway interest.

116

The German officials, who were moved by our misfortune, advised us to get out in Kibart on the Russian side of the border and contact a Mr. Schidorsky, the woman continues. And he actually turned out to be our savior. He gave us passes to Eydtkuhnen, where his brother headed up a relief organization for emigrants. The good man, a Jew, gave us lodging in his own home for many days, despite our wretched appearance. Then he arranged our crossing to Germany. We got on the train in Eydtkuhnen, and were in Berlin sometime around evening. I still get dizzy when I think how we whirled through that city. It seemed like we kept going faster and faster.

The woman's breast protrudes, white and plump, from her dress. The child's nose makes a small dent in it. He drinks quickly, with his eyes shut. His little Adam's apple bobs up and down.

Our train suddenly stopped on a remote field, opposite a building that stood by itself in a large yard. We had to get out. Children cried out for their parents, parents for their children. It was utter chaos. Our baggage was thrown carelessly into a pile in one corner of the yard; Germans dressed in white shouted out orders — *schnell, schnell*, quickly, quickly — and we all followed them like obedient children.

No wonder everything that happened thickened into a plot of robbers and murderers in some people's heads! Finally, they took us to a place where there was only a single house to be seen. They took away our belongings and separated us from our friends. A man inspected us like he wanted to determine our current market value. Strange-looking people drove us here and there as if we were dumb, helpless animals. Children were bawling, and we were crammed into a small room where a great big cauldron of water was boiling on top of the stove. They took away our clothes and smeared us with some slippery substance that had us fearing for the worst. Without any warning whatsoever, warm water poured down on us from showers. Then we were herded into another room where we sat huddled in wool blankets until they brought in large sacks which they emptied on to the floor — it was our clothing. All we could make out was clouds of steam and orders to get dressed. *Schnell, schnell.* We have to pick our clothes out of that tangled mass and meanwhile, the steam is blinding us. We practically suffocate; we ask the attendants for more time, but they don't care. *Schnell, schnell,* or you'll miss the train. Oh, so they're not going to kill us. They're just getting us ready for the rest of the journey, they're just making sure we don't have any dangerous diseases.

When there were outbreaks of cholera in Polotzk, which happened once or twice every generation, we didn't make such a big to-do about it like these Germans. Whoever died from it was buried, and whoever survived went to the synagogue to pray. We felt offended by the way the Germans treated us. My mother almost died of cholera once, but they gave her a new name, a lucky one that saved her life; she was just a little girl when that happened. Now, none of us were even sick, but all these policemen and nurses were screaming orders at us and making sure to keep at a distance from us, like we were lepers they weren't allowed to come into contact with.

The infant lets go of the breast. His head slowly tilts backwards; he has fallen asleep. A white drop clings to the big brown nipple.

We reached Hamburg in the early morning hours, following a long night in overcrowded compartments. They took us to a strange-looking carriage that was long and narrow and high; it was pulled by two horses and steered by a mute driver. They shoved us into this carriage and threw our baggage in after us. That was the beginning of a long journey through Hamburg. It lasted for hours, and still the horses kept going, and still not a word of explanation. We were strangers to the city, and the coachman knew it. He could drive us anywhere he felt like — how were we to know? We were overcome by the same fear we felt in Berlin.

Our mysterious trip finally ended on the outskirts of the city, where we were all lined up again, interrogated, disinfected, tagged, and then shut in this place. Once again, we suspected we were the victims of a conspiracy to extort money from us. As was the case when we were cleaned before, we had to pay a fee here, too. But we didn't have any money left. They didn't believe us, and so, as the final crowning humiliation, we were subjected to a body-search.

And now we are sitting here in this prison, behind high walls and barred windows, crammed by the hundreds into half a dozen numbered divisions, where there's a roll call every morning and every evening, just like in jail.

The woman hasn't noticed that her baby stopped nursing. Her white breast projects from her dress. It occurs to Daniel that he will sleep next to his mother tonight. The woman feels his eyes upon her and pulls up her dress.

The *Saxonia* bunkers coal and water and unloads her mixed cargo. The stevedores work their way further and further belowdecks, down companionways and into cabins that are stacked to the ceiling, down into the 'tween-decks, where the steerage passengers will spend the voyage. Little by little, the alleyways become empty, and the three-tiered rows of bunk beds fastened to the walls become visible, as do the tables and benches stacked one upon the other.

Skat players are used to kibitzers; that's because there is an unwritten law that allows anyone to be a spectator. This meant that the three men hardly noticed Mr. Nussbaum at first; but when they finally did, they *really* noticed him. Klaus Groth is just about to play the ace of spades. His hand flies up in the air in order to slam the card down on the table in triumph, when all of a sudden, there is barking.

His hand holding the card hangs there in midair. They're still gazing down at the seven of clubs and the ten of clubs on the table; then they look at each other. What was that?

They look at Mr. Nussbaum, and once again, there is barking. Mr. Nussbaum tilts his head to one side and barks. Three times. Then he looks at them in embarrassment and smiles apologetically. Slowly and ever so cautiously, Klaus Groth lowers his hand with the ace of spades to the table. They lean back. They've had a fright. They think a bit.

Wouldn't you like to take a seat? says Robert Benz, as if that could buy him some time.

Gladly, says Mr. Nussbaum gratefully, and swiftly sits down.

Do you want to play cards with us? asks Klaus Groth.

Thank you, says Mr. Nussbaum. But I am incapable of comprehending the game.

They stare straight ahead a while longer. They think some more. Then Simon Kantor resolutely shuffles the cards and deals.

Mr. Nussbaum sits next to Robert Benz. But he only takes a peek at Benz's cards now and then. His eyelids begin to droop; he sinks down in his seat a little, but starts up over and over again, opening his eyes wide every time. The intervals in between become longer and longer, however, and finally, it can't be overlooked anymore: He has fallen asleep.

And that is when they notice the swarm of smirking children lurking in the doorway. Klaus Groth only has to turn his gaze on them and slowly rise from the table for them to dash off, screeching. He lowers his frame on to the bench again. So that was the explanation for Mr. Nussbaum's bustling haste: He was on the run. Wherever he happened to turn up, children were hot on his heels. The human dog.

They keep playing until the attendants announce lights out; then they wake him. Time to go to bed, Mr. Nussbaum.

Many times now, Robert Benz had reached the point where he was about to give up and turn himself in. I'll do a couple years time and then start over again, he said to himself. And you really think you'll come out of jail the same way you went in? he objected in reply. You won't even be able to recognize yourself afterwards. And who's going to give a jailbird work? Who'll still let him sit down at the same table with them? The real punishment isn't the time in prison; it's the years that follow — the rest of one's life.

Nevertheless, the temptation to run to the nearest police station grew. Until he met Karoline Ebel. Ever since then, he has been a happy man, and now, together with her, he even thinks he can take on America.

It is forbidden to approach the perimeter wall, and it is especially forbidden to pull oneself up on it in order to have a look at the port. They make an exception for Groth. Not just because he is German, but also because he does not make any attempt to peer over it. All he wants to do is stand there and listen to the harbor noises. He can still turn back. He has read the Socialists' newspaper attentively enough to know what awaits a proletarian like him in America. And yet. What? He listens.

Skat, then, is good for many things. Even for blocking out music, or a certain kind of music. For that evening, an accordion begins to play somewhere in the huts. It has a decidedly epic vein; a penchant for telling long, complex stories that take place on wide plains, or along the banks of a broad, slow-moving river, and sometimes in open birch groves. Clouds, and many times the moon, too, play an important role. Conversations die down then, and eyes stare off blankly into space. Skat, then — a complicated Null Ouvert or a Clubs game without 4, for instance — is good for that.

Once the cards are dealt, Mr. Nussbaum is never far away. It seems it is his way of being tactful that he only approaches them on the pretext of kibitzing. Even though he himself admitted that he doesn't know the first thing about skat and is not capable of understanding the game, he follows it with interest.

They act as if he is the fourth man whose turn it is to sit out a round. When one of them makes an especially shrewd play, he darts a slyly conspirative glance his way; or, when he's won his hand, a triumphant one. On those occasions, Mr. Nussbaum is happy for the winner. Sometimes he cannot help barking.

His sister has already gone on ahead of him to New York, he relates. She's waiting for him there. Her name is Käthe.

May I ask where you are from? inquires Robert Benz.

Mr. Nussbaum undoes the top button of his waistcoat and pulls out a pouch he wears around his neck.

Everything about Nussbaum is in here, he says. He extends the bag to Benz.

Go ahead and take it, he exclaims. The pouch is hanging by a cord that encircles Mr. Nussbaum's neck.

Hesitantly, as if afraid he would have to touch Mr. Nussbaum himself, Benz's hand inches toward the leather pouch. But then, hesitant no longer, Benz scoots over next to him, snaps open the bag, and removes its contents. He turns pages; reads; then he returns everything to the pouch and snaps it shut.

Thank you, he says, ill at ease.

Mr. Nussbaum puts the leather pouch back under his waistcoat.

I must be on my way, he says. I'm much too late already.

He scurries off, and it must be said that he wears his little paunch well.

No one speaks for a while.

He's from Hirschheim in the Palatinate, says Benz. He's got his passport and the ticket with him. And nothing else.

The next day, something gargantuan slowly moves out in front of the barred windows; it is the superstructure of a steamship. The *Saxonia* is being towed to the America quay.

Cleaning crews swarm up the gangway. Vehicles with long blocks of ice drive up. They are being pulled by heavy horses whose straw-colored manes have been plaited into braids and adorned with ribbons and little bells. Men in leather aprons lift the whitish ice blocks on to their shoulders and carry them up the gangplank. Belowdecks, the steerage area is being cleaned; the heads emptied; benches and tables set up; mattresses laid out on the berths.

The noise level in the huts suddenly increased. Many people had to spend two weeks in them; a length of time stretching out so endlessly that they hardly believed they would ever get any further. Daniel calculates the number of hours left until departure. He draws a line for each hour. When one has gone by, he draws another line through it. That just makes the time pass even more slowly, his father tells him. The accordion now wallows in melancholy, making it even more draining on the listeners by adding a dash of wistful irony. They up the ante from a tenth of a penny to a whole penny. That helps them concentrate.

And your sister is waiting for you in New York? asks Simon Kantor.

Yes, she'll be there to meet the train is what they told me.

Is what they told you. Faced with Mr. Nussbaum's friendly smile, Simon Kantor lowers his eyes.

Has she been in New York long?

She went there just four weeks ago. I don't understand why she didn't tell me about going there. She simply disappeared. But I'm sure she'll explain everything to me in New York.

Did you live with her?

Always. She took care of me. Without her...well, that just would never do.

He can't help but bark. Very hard and for a very long time; it is such that they have to hold on to him. Afterwards, he is completely exhausted.

You know what? says Robert Benz. We're going to bed now. It'll be lights out soon anyhow. You can have my bed; that way, you can lie between the two of them, and they'll watch out for you. I'll look for another one.

On the second-to-the-last day, they start playing skat already in the morning.

Do you think this sister in New York really exists? says Klaus Groth.

I'd like to know what happened four weeks ago, says Benz. He said she just disappeared then.

She's dead, says Simon Kantor. There's nobody waiting for him in New York.

If he has one of his fits on Ellis Island, says Klaus Groth, they'll send him back.

Hopefully he'll have one, says Robert Benz.

Have a seat, Mr. Nussbaum, Simon Kantor calls out. We've been expecting you.

This place is impossible, says Mr. Nussbaum. One can't even wash oneself properly. And it is imperative that I change my clothes. But someone stole my suitcase and my coat and my hat.

I'll bet you came here on the train, says Robert Benz.

Yes, I did indeed. Mr. Meiser, our sexton, brought me and left me here. Wasn't that nice of him? The city even sacrificed all the revenue from the dog tax so I could go to Käthe.

When he leaves to make one of his rounds, they decide to use the skat pool to buy him a hat and coat from the clothing shop at the entrance to the huts.

The next-to-last day. Daniel can now count the hours remaining until they board the ship on four hands. Late that afternoon, a hackney stops at the gangway of the *Saxonia*. Albert Werth gets out. He ascends the gangplank; the coachman follows with two suitcases. He couldn't stand it at home anymore. It suddenly dawns on him that upon his return, he will have to get his own apartment. He gets settled in his cabin with relish. He is looking forward to the coming weeks with an intensity he last experienced as a pupil looking forward to the holidays.

It is one in the morning. Tatlin stands in front of the *Saxonia*. She'll put out to sea tomorrow at twelve noon. The passengers will board her around ten, and they will go on board via the gangway that has already been laid out, but which comes to an end up above at a locked door. He won't be able to use that route, because tomorrow morning, three men will be standing there where the gangway begins, and they will be waiting for him. Therefore, he has to be on the ship beforehand. He looks up the huge steel ship's wall that looms before him, black as the night. How is he supposed to get up there?

Roll call is at six a.m., after breakfast. Names begin to be shouted. Each man or woman called presents their identification papers and is then waved, together with children and other relatives, into the dining room, where everyone has to wait.

More than six hundred names have to be called. Shortly before ten, the procedure is over. The doors are opened and the procession makes its way toward the *Saxonia*, with HAPAG officials leading the way. They all have to walk up the one gangway. That is going to take a while. From the promenade deck, Albert Werth looks down on the waiting masses and on the thin line of people making their way up the gangplank. After watching this for a bit, he returns to his cabin.

Just before noon, the siren of the *Saxonia* emits a muffled, hoarse call. Werth goes back outside to observe them putting off from their berth. There are only a handful of people still waiting in front of the gangway. In the end, only the HAPAG officials are left, and three men in civilian clothes.

In addition to Albert Werth, someone else is observing them. From a lifeboat, to be precise. It is covered over with a tarpaulin that is attached to the boat with leather fasteners. At one particular spot, two of the fasteners have been undone and the tarpaulin has been lifted ever so slightly. Two ice-blue, mocking eyes peer through the narrow gap. Tatlin giggles.

The command to haul in the gangway has been given. Two sailors are getting ready to carry it out when a hackney approaches at a trot that is practically a gallop and stops. A nun leaps out and runs toward the gangplank with vestments flying in the wind.

Albert Werth gives a shout and starts to wave. Hello! he yells enthusiastically, and he almost jumped for joy. But Sister Alma naturally has better things to do than look up at him. She has to get up the gangway before it goes slack. The two sailors have grabbed her suitcases from the coachman's hands and are running up the gangplank with them behind her.

As it turns out, it takes another hour before the *Saxonia* is towed free, out of the port, and floating on the current. Sometimes the wind forces the smoke from the funnels down on to the deck. Tiny particles of soot settle on coats and hats; when their owners attempt to brush them off, they leave behind fine black streaks.

On the banks of the Elbe, the white of the villas shines forth from between trees in the park. The wind picks up. It blows stiffly up the Elbe, coming over the water from the west; it's not like the wind that blows inland. Off Brunsbüttel, the river broadens; the shores can barely be made out now.

Dr. Albert Werth's presence is requested at the captain's dinner this evening. He will try to ask Sister Alma to attend it with him. But there's still time until then. By then, the *Saxonia* will be on the high seas, small and, in the end, indistinguishable from the gray of the falling dusk.